Martha Mayhem

and the Witch from the Ditch

Love and thanks to the Incredible Owens
(John, Joan, James, Jesse and Lily),
the Jolly Johns (Katie, Dan, Jack, Mollie and Tillie),
and to my Spectacularly Supportive Stephen

First published in Great Britain in 2017 by
PICCADILLY PRESS
80–81 Wimpole St, London W1G 9RE
www.piccadillypress.co.uk

Text copyright © Joanne Owen, 2017
Illustrations copyright © Tony Ross, 2017

A CIP catalogue record for this book is available from the British Library.

ISBN: 978-1-84812-536-0
also available as an ebook

1

Printed and bound by Clays Ltd, St Ives Plc

Piccadilly Press is an imprint of Bonnier Zaffre Ltd,
a Bonnier Publishing company
www.bonnierpublishing.co.uk

Martha Mayhem

and the Witch from the Ditch

JOANNE OWEN

ILLUSTRATED BY TONY ROSS

Piccadilly
PRESS

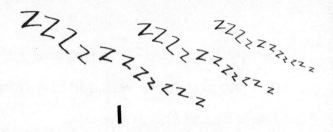

Martha Mayhem and the Mysterious Moonlit Moans

It was almost midnight on the eve of Halloween Eve. The air was frosty, the moon was as full and fat as a ball of creamy cheese, and all was calm in the village of Cherry Hillsbottom. You could practically see a string of silent zzzzzzzs rising from the roofs as everyone slept as quiet and cosy as hamsters in a huddle. Well, it wasn't *completely* quiet. On the far edge of the village, out beyond Raspberry Road and

Lumpy Lane, and past Foxglove Field, an odd buzzing noise was bursting from the house at the end of the lane.

In the attic room of that house at the end of the lane, Martha Mayhem flipped over for about the fiftieth time that night, releasing another stream of buzzes from her busy brain. *Buzz-buzz-buzz*, it went, like a swarm of extremely excited bees. *Buzz-buzzbuzzzzzzz*, over and over again. It usually

took three stories, one hot chocolate and counting 352 goats for Martha to fall asleep, but tonight, after reading eight stories, slurping three hot chocolates and counting at least 521 goats, 683 hummingbirds and 53 whales, she was *still* buzzing and fizzing, and for very good reason. And this very good reason was that Martha couldn't stop thinking about how close Halloween was. It was one of her favourite days of the year.

BUZZZZZZ   BUZZZZZZZZZ

BUZZZZZ

There was always a big party in Foxglove Field, and all the villagers dressed up and played ghoulish games while filling their faces with fiendish food.

Martha had already laid out her witch's costume on the end of her bed, and it seemed to be calling to her. *Put me on, put me on*, it called. The spots on her red-and-purple polka-dot dress seemed to be dancing in the moonlight, urging her to *put me on, put me on*. The stripes on her black-and-purple tights seemed to be spinning around, urging her to *put me on, put me on*. And so it was with the silver stars stuck to her raggedy red cape, and the purple glitter on her shoes. *Put me on, put me on*, they whispered. Thinking it would be very rude to ignore her costume's calls, Martha scrambled down her bed and changed into her outfit faster than a snake slithering down a slippery pole. Then she raced to the mirror and squashed her hat onto her curly-whirly hair. It had taken her approximately twenty-three hours to make her hat from a sheet of card and pieces of silver paper she'd cut into moons. But Martha didn't mind how long it had taken, because she LOVED making things, like witches' hats and lists, and friends and scrambled eggs.

And sometimes Martha made mayhem, whether she liked it or not. In fact, that's why her best friend Jack had named her 'Martha Mayhem' when her actual name was Martha *May*.

For example, one recent pandemonium-packed incident had involved Martha roller-skating to school. Roller-skating to school doesn't *sound* particularly pandemonium-packed, but in Martha's world one thing almost always led to another at considerable speed — much like the wheels of her roller skates. In this particular incident, Martha skidded on a stone, lost control, whizzed round a corner and collided with a poodle. But it wasn't just any poodle. The poodle belonged to her teacher, Miss Parpwell, and unfortunately the shock of the collision caused the poodle to poop on Miss Parpwell's shoes. Even more unfortunately, the shock of having her shoes pooped on made Miss Parpwell shriek like a banshee, which in turn upset the poodle, which in turn made Martha give it a great big hug, which in turn made the poodle leap onto Martha with considerable force.

As a result of this, Martha careered into Miss Parpwell and the incident came to a sorry conclusion when Miss Parpwell was sent hurtling down Raspberry Road like a human rolling pin and had to take a week off school to recover. So you see, in Martha's world, something as innocent-seeming as a stray stone might lead to all manner of mayhem.

While Martha was admiring how wonderfully witchy she looked, she heard a mysterious noise coming from outside.

Aaquwwwww– ooooooh– aaahhhooo ww!

moaned the mysterious noise.

'Cripes!' cried Martha. 'What kind of MONSTROUS creature would make a sound like *that*?'

 Martha ran to the window and peered outside, but all she saw was the fat, creamy moon beaming down on the monster-less meadow behind the house. Feeling puzzled, Martha climbed back into bed, still wearing her witch's costume (firstly because she hadn't heard it call, *take me off, take me off,* and secondly because she loved it so much). Then she tried, once again, to sleep, this time counting a collection of creepy creatures making mysterious moaning noises.

2

The Hog in the Bog

A-a-a-a-a-choooooo!

Martha Mayhem woke with an enormous sneeze blasting from her nose and a great grin on her face (despite being sneezy, she *still* felt bright and breezy, because today actually *was* Halloween Eve).

'Bless you, my Bouncy Bubble!' came a cheery voice from downstairs. It was Professor Gramps, Martha's granddad, who looked after her while her mum (Professor

Margarita May) and dad (Professor Magnus May) worked abroad. Her mum and dad were both Professors of Creeping Creatures, which meant they took lots of trips to tropical places so they could research things like tiny exotic reptiles and giant exotic millipedes.

Martha wasn't *entirely* sure what Professor Gramps was a professor of. It seemed most likely that he was a Professor of Everything because he knew ALL kinds of fascinating facts, like where to find the world's biggest butterfly (Papua New Guinea), and when toilets were invented (2800 BC), and which birds are the ONLY kind that can fly backwards (hummingbirds). In fact, he even mumbled fascinating facts in his sleep. Martha was very fond of Gramps because he called her names like 'Bouncy Bubble', and because his favourite food was ginger-and-rhubarb jam, and because he was (most probably) a Professor of Everything.

'Ready for breakfast, Prickly Pineapple?'

'Coming, Gramps!'

'If you get your skates on, you'll be just in time for school,' replied the Professor. 'Not literally, of course,' he added. 'Not after that palaver with Miss Parpwell's poodle.'

At Gramps's mention of school (and the poodle palaver), Martha's grin turned into a grimace, because that meant she had to change from her Halloween costume into her itchy uniform. She especially disliked her itchy, grey school tights, which made her feel like she was trapped inside a toilet roll. After dragging on her scratchy, itchy uniform, she plonked herself in front of her dressing table and twirled her messy hair into two twiggy plaits before stomping down to the kitchen.

A-a-a-a-a-choooooooo! she erupted.

'Bless your blustery beak!' said Professor Gramps. 'You look like you haven't slept a wink. Did your cold keep you awake, Sneezerella?'

'It wasn't the sneezes, Gramps.'

'Then what was it, Sniffle Snitch?' asked Professor Gramps. 'Come to think of it, you look like you've seen a ghost.'

'Well, I did hear some mysterious moans coming from the meadow last night. They sounded something like this:

Aaquwwwww – oooooh – aaahhhooo ww!

she demonstrated. 'What could it have been, Gramps?'

'Hmm,' said Professor Gramps thoughtfully. 'Perhaps it was an owl, or a bat,' he suggested. 'Nothing to worry about, most likely, but I'll be sure to keep an ear out for whatever it was.'

He wiggled his ears to prove it. 'Now eat your breakfast, Turnip Tusks. I'll be in my library if you need me.'

After crunching through a big bowl of cereal, all the time wondering if the peculiar noises were or weren't something she should worry about, Martha ran outside to the meadow.

'Morning, Elvis!' she called. Elvis was Martha's pet hog. Well, he wasn't *exactly* hers. She and Gramps were looking after him for their friend Tacita Truelace. He'd only arrived at Tacita's at the end of the summer but had grown so much since then that he couldn't really fit in the tiny garden outside Tacita's tearoom any more.

And even though he'd only been staying with Martha and Professor Gramps for a few weeks, Martha already couldn't imagine life without him.

'Elvis?' She frowned. Something wasn't right. Not right at all. Elvis always trotted up to her as soon as she came to say good morning, but today the handsome hog was heaped in a hump in the bog at the back of his pen. His usually perky tail was as floppy as a soggy fish finger, and his long, curly eyelashes had wilted like wet spider's legs.

'Gramps, come quick!' called Martha. 'There's something wrong with Elvis!' She climbed into the pen and gently stroked the sprouts of spiky bristles that ran along his back.

'What is it, my Merry Martian?' asked Professor Gramps as he emerged from his library, which was a yellow shed with green curtains and a red door. Since Professor Gramps usually wore a mustard-coloured suit with a green waistcoat and red tie, he usually looked a lot like his library shed.

'It's Elvis,' Martha replied, her voice faint. 'He looks . . . droopy.'

Professor Gramps rushed towards them, releasing a little groan with every creak of his ancient bones (he had a different groan for every bone). He joined Martha inside the pen and examined Elvis from the tip of his snout to the end of his floppy tail. 'Hmm,' he said, scratching his chin. 'I do believe you're right. He's as droopy as a dewdrop. Perhaps he's caught your cold.'

'Shall I fetch him something warm to wear?' Martha suggested, imagining how snug Elvis would feel (and how smart he would look) with a bright bobble hat on his head.

'Let's see how he goes, eh?' Professor Gramps winked. 'He might be back to his happy, hoggy self by lunchtime. I'll research peculiar porcine behaviour while you're at school. I'll be very thorough, don't you worry. I'll go the whole *hog*, so to speak.'

'This is not the time for making jokes, Gramps,' said Martha, folding her arms. 'Elvis might be *seriously* ill.'

'I'm sorry, my dear,' said Professor Gramps, 'but let's not get our knickers in a twist before we know what's wrong with him.'

The thought of Professor Gramps wearing a pair of twisty knickers was just TOO MUCH and Martha EXPLODED with the kind of snort-off-your-snout laugh that's impossible to control.

She was laughing so much she didn't notice Elvis heaving himself up, as slow as a snail, as if a great weight — like a house — was on his back. He stretched out his neck and released an incredible moaning noise that sounded something like this:

Aaquwwwww– oOooooh– aaahhhooo ww!

'That's what I heard last night, Gramps!' yelled Martha, stopping mid-snort, her eyes almost popping out of her head. 'It was Elvis! Whatever's wrong with him?'

'I can't say for certain at the moment,' said Professor Gramps. 'But don't worry, I'll be sure to investigate.'

'Maybe I should stay home today, Gramps,' Martha wondered. 'I could take care of Elvis and help you with your investigation.'

'That's very kind of you, Treacle Toes, but I don't want us to get in trouble with Miss Parpwell. I'll do everything I can to make him better. He'll be right in no time, I promise.'

'OK, Gramps,' said Martha Mayhem. She gave Elvis a big hug, hoping with all her heart that her Professor of Everything was right.

3

The Witch from the Ditch

Martha Mayhem normally loved her journey to school through Cherry Hillsbottom, especially on bright autumn mornings like this one when the ground was crunchy with leaves and Foxglove Field sparkled with frost and you could make clouds with your breath. But today wasn't a normal day. Today, as Martha mooched miserably down Lumpy Lane, all she could think about was poor Elvis. She wondered when he'd be back to doing what he loved, like snuffling fruity roots and wallowing in wet mud. Martha was so fond of Elvis she would do *anything* for him. For example, she didn't even mind cleaning out his (sometimes poopy) pen. She was seriously considering turning back and running home to look after him when an unexpected sound interrupted her thoughts.

'**Heee-**eeeelp **me!**' said the sound.

Martha Mayhem froze. She'd never heard anything like it. It was part wail, part whisper, and both parts sounded extremely sad.

'Please **heee-**eeeelp **me!**' the voice repeated. 'I've been locked in here for an eternity.'

'That sounds like an *awfully* long time,' said Martha. 'Of course I'll help, but I'm afraid I can't see you. Where *exactly* are you?'

'In the gate,' whisper-wailed the voice. 'Come closer.'

Martha had never heard of anyone being locked inside a gate before, but she moved closer to get a better look.

'I'm afraid I still can't see any . . . A-a-a-a-a-c hoooooooo! Martha sneezed with such ferocious force that the gate blew open and she shot through it like a circus performer being fired from a cannon.

Feeling relieved that she
hadn't been propelled
to the outer edges of the
universe (or at least to Plumtum
Town, which was the next village
along from Cherry Hillsbottom), Martha
turned her attention back to the gate.

She examined it so closely that she didn't notice a patch of grey cloud drifting up and over the gate, and she didn't notice what was going on right beside her . . .

'Argh-*argh*-ooo-*yu-yu*-ee**eee**!'

screeched a voice.

Martha jumped. The voice was prickly and scratchy and reminded her of her toilet-roll tights, or Elvis's back bristles, or her best friend Jack trying to play the violin. It sounded nothing like the sad wail-whisper.

'Hurry up and help me, you nincompoop! I'm trapped in the ditch!'

Wondering how many more strange voices she was going to hear in a single day, Martha looked down. **'Yikessssss!'** she squealed at the sight of a pair of twiggy legs twitching in a ditch just the other side of the gate. The twiggy legs were attached to a bony body, and the bony body was attached to a messy-haired head.

'Ooh, I like your witch's costume!' Martha beamed. 'It's *practically* the same as mine, except I don't have ENORMOUS puffy purple polka-dot knickers to wear over my stripy tights. Couldn't you wait for Halloween either? I was so excited I wore my costume to bed last night.'

'This isn't a *costume*,' snorted the wiggly woman. 'These are my most special clothes.'

'I'm sorry,' said Martha Mayhem. She hadn't meant to cause offence, and she did think that the woman's outfit *was* pretty special. 'Wait a minute . . .' Martha's heart began to beat **boom-boom-boom** in her chest, and her eyes began to **BOGGLE** as An Incredible Thought struck her. 'Cripes!' she gasped. 'If this isn't a costume, are you . . . are you a *real* witch? An *actual witch*?

Do all *actual witches* wear knickers like that? And was it you making that whispering, wailing noise? I never imagined witches sounded like that. And where's your broomstick?'

Martha knew she was probably asking too many questions at once, but it was impossible to choose which one to ask first. She needed to know the answers to *all* of them.

'Of *course* I'm an ACTUAL witch,' huffed the witch. 'And I suggest you stop being rude about my knickers. As well as being fashionable, they have an immensely important function. In fact, they're the reason I don't need a broomstick. Now stop jabbering and help me up!'

Martha was very keen to know what knickers had to do with broomsticks, but she didn't want to make this *actual witch* any angrier, so she hitched up her itchy skirt, kneeled down in the ditch and untangled the witch's spindly legs from the brambles.

'I wouldn't like to be you,' snapped the witch, springing to her feet. 'Not for all the magical brews and supernatural stews in the entire universe. You have done A Dreadful Deed.'

Martha fidgeted with her fingers. She didn't *think* she'd done anything dreadful. At least, she hadn't *meant* to do anything dreadful. 'What Dreadful Deed do you mean?'

The witch from the ditch snorted.

'I MEAN you released the ghoul from the gate. The force of your sneeze blasted it out, and the gust from the ghoul sent me flying into this ditch while I was innocently walking through this field.'

'A *ghoul*?' Martha gasped. 'An *actual* ghoul? Do *they* really exist too? Hang on . . .' Martha paused to let her tongue catch up with her buzzing brain. 'Was *that* what I heard? Was it a *ghoul* asking for my help? It sounded awfully sad.'

'Are all humans as foolish as you?' snapped the witch, scratching her pointy nose. There were four hairs on the end of it, Martha noticed, each of them waggling in the wind like the legs of an angry beetle. 'Yes, there *was* a ghoul,' the witch went on.

'A ghastly ghoul. It must have been locked inside the gate to stop it from doing any more silly hauntings. That's why they're usually locked in gates. Everyone knows that.'

'Oh,' said Martha. 'I'm sorry. I didn't *mean* to do anything wrong, and I'm afraid I didn't know that about ghouls. Shall we put it back inside together?' she offered helpfully.

'You can't just put them back inside. At least, I don't think you can. I can't be expected to remember everything I learned at Madam Malenka's Academy of Enchantment, can I?' replied the witch unhelpfully. 'And besides, did you see where it went?'

Martha shook her head.

'So how are we supposed to get it back inside if we can't find it, Smarty-pants? It could be lurking anywhere, ready to come for you at any moment. If I were you, I'd get out of here as fast as your legs will carry you. I'm off to find my little sister. Actually, do you know her? She's supposed to live around here. And do you know Helga-Holga?'

'I'm afraid I don't know anyone called Helga-Holga,' said Martha. 'And I know everyone here. Your sister must live somewhere else.'

'Helga-Holga isn't my sister,' scoffed the witch from the ditch. 'My sister is Tacita Truelace, and she *definitely* lives in Cherry Hillsbum. This *is* Cherry Hillsbum, isn't it?'

'Hills*BUM*!' Martha exploded into giggles. 'You mean Hills*BOTTOM*, not Hills*BUM*!!!'

'I don't know why you're wasting all your energy on being silly when a ghoul is going to get you,' snapped the witch. 'This isn't a laughing matter. Do you or do you not know Tacita Truelace?'

Martha Mayhem immediately pulled her face into a serious expression, as if she were wearing a mask of her head teacher's face. 'You're right,' she said.

34

'I don't imagine having a ghoul after you *is* a laughing matter. I know Miss Truelace. She runs the tearoom down there, on Raspberry Road. But is she *really* your sister?' Martha frowned. 'You don't look at all like each other. Is *she* a witch too?'

But the witch from the ditch wasn't listening. The witch from the ditch had shot down Lumpy Lane so fast she was already out of sight.

4

In which
Martha Mayhem Gets in a Flap

'WAIT! Come back!' Martha yelled after the witch from the ditch. She sprinted down Lumpy Lane (backwards, in case the ghoul from the gate tried to creep up behind her), making a list of important questions in her head as she went:

1) Is this witch from the ditch really Miss Truelace's sister?

2a) Is a ghoul from the gate really going to get me?

2b) If the ghoul does get me, what EXACTLY will it do?

3) What do knickers have to do with broomsticks?

Breathless, Martha reached Tacita Truelace's Tearoom, but to her surprise it was still closed, so she dashed to Tacita's house, which was just next door. 'Miss Truelace?' she called through the letterbox. 'Are you all right? Did your sister find you?'

Just then, she felt something tickle her legs through her (toilet-roll) tights. *'Not the ghoul, not the ghoul, not the ghoul . . .'* she whispered. Taking a deep breath, Martha looked down. 'Trinket!' It was Miss Truelace's cat. 'Thank goodness! I thought you were the ghoul. Where's Miss Truelace, Trinks? Why isn't she answering?'

Trinket licked her paws elegantly and slunk indoors through her cat flap, which gave Martha an *excellent* idea. She stretched out in front of the door and wiggled through after the cat.

And then she got stuck.

Martha breathed in as hard as she could, but that made no difference. She was well and truly trapped, wedged halfway in, halfway out, wishing she hadn't eaten such a big bowl of cereal for breakfast. Then, as if being trapped in a cat flap wasn't bad enough, she heard something that could only mean one thing: *everything* was about to get much worse.

'Martha May, get up this instant! What on EARTH do you think you're doing?'

It was Miss Parpwell, who wasn't the kind of person you would want to find you stuck in a cat flap. In fact, she wasn't the kind of person you would want to find you doing anything unusual. She was a mean,  moody lady with a mean, moody face. Her lips turned down, as if she'd never smiled in her entire life, and her nose turned up, as if it was trying to stretch away from a truly terrible smell.

Miss Parpwell liked impossible maths, puzzles and peace and quiet. Miss Parpwell did not like overactive imaginations and noise. Miss Parpwell *definitely* did not like any kind of mayhem.

'Well?' parped Miss Parpwell. 'Has the cat got your tongue?'

'Not *exactly*,' said Martha, her voice muffled from being on the other side of the door. 'But this cat flap does have me trapped. I don't suppose you've seen a witch anywhere?'

'Stop talking nonsense and GET UP!'

'I'm afraid I can't do that,' Martha explained. 'I'm stuck.'

Huffing and puffing like she'd just run a marathon, Miss Parpwell took hold of Martha's feet and tugged on them until she came free from the flap.

'Thanks, Miss Parpwell. It was becoming pretty tricky to breathe.'

'Quiet! Or I shall be forced to have EXTREMELY stern words with your grandfather.'

Martha Mayhem did not want anyone to have EXTREMELY stern words with Professor Gramps, especially not Miss Parpwell, so she sealed her lips and followed Miss Parpwell to school, as silent as a mouse on a secret mission.

5

The Classroom Clanger

While Martha managed to keep her lips sealed for the rest of the journey, Miss Parpwell's down turned lips didn't stop moving. She wouldn't stop going on about what pests cats were, particularly in relation to pet poodles. Martha was glad when they arrived at the school.

'Sit down,' ordered Miss Parpwell when they reached the classroom. 'And do NOT say a word until I say you can.'

Martha did as she was told and sat down at her desk next to Jack. Her fizz had gone flat, like a bottle of sparkly drink with its lid left off. For now, she was plain old Martha May.

'What's grey and itchy and lives in the bathroom?' asked Jack, with a cheeky twinkle in his eyes.

Martha twitched her nose like a nervous rabbit, hoping this would tell Jack that something **EXTRAORDINARY** had happened. She couldn't bear not being able to tell him. They'd been best friends for as long as Martha could remember. In fact, they'd been best friends since *before* either of them could remember. That is to say, they'd first encountered one another before they were even born, when they were both no bigger than bite-sized beans in their mums' tums. According to Martha's mum, every time they met as little beans Martha would jiggle and wiggle in a way that felt exactly like a jumping jelly bean. And according to Jack's mum, every time they met as little beans Jack would jump and jolt in a way that felt like he was an actual jack-in-the-box.

'I asked you a question.' Jack frowned. 'What's grey and itchy and lives in the bathroom?'

Martha twitched her nose again. She felt like an overblown balloon that was about to **BURST**. But since she could feel Miss Parpwell's eyes burning into her like laser beams, Martha kept quiet, hoping an opportunity to speak would present itself sometime soon.

'Aren't you going to answer?' asked Jack. 'It's YOU in your toilet-roll tights, of course!'

But Martha said nothing. She didn't even laugh, which wasn't at all like her. She *always* laughed at Jack's jokes, even when they weren't funny. In fact, it was Martha who'd named him 'Jack Joke'.

His real name was Jack Sherbet, but some people (well, one person: Sally Sweetpea) called him 'Sausage Fingers' (because his dad, Herbert Sherbet, was a butcher), and other people (for example, Nathaniel Hackett Crisp Packet) called him 'Scrambled Egg Head' (because his messy yellow hair looked like scrambled egg).

Someone else (Jack's dad) sometimes called him 'Jack Jitter' because, while he was almost as brave as a buccaneer exploring snake-infested jungles when it came to telling jokes or performing on the football pitch, when it came to other things, like monsters or sleeping in the dark, Jack had a tendency to jitter with fright.

'What's wrong?' asked Jack. Martha's strange behaviour was beginning to worry him. 'And why did you come in with Parp Smell?'

Martha glanced up. Both of Miss Parpwell's eyes were busy checking her fingernails, which meant Martha had an opportunity to speak.

'I'm not allowed to talk,' she whispered, 'but something **INCREDIBLY** exciting has happened. Something *scary*.'

'Speak up,' said Jack. 'What's hairy?'

It was then that Martha Mayhem actually *did* burst. She just couldn't help it. '*Scary!* Not *HAIRY!*' she spluttered.

'Martha May! Stop making that horrific

hullabaloo!' parped Miss Parpwell. 'Everyone settle down and open your story-writing books,' she ordered.

A snigger came from the girl sitting in front of Martha. With a sweeping flick of her golden hair, the girl – Sally Sweetpea – turned around and stuck out her tongue. Martha had to try very hard not to say anything or make a face back.

Sally Sweetpea and Martha Mayhem were the opposite of being as alike as two peas in a pod. That is to say, they were nothing like each other. Or, to put it another way, they were as alike as a pea and a peacock, or a pencil and a penguin. For example, Sally Sweetpea's hair was always neat, she *never* felt like a toilet-roll tube and she didn't like handsome hogs or finding out fascinating facts. But, while she was sweet by name, Sally was **SOUR** by nature. In fact, Jack Joke had invented the nickname 'Sally *Sour*pea' for her, and that was what both he and Martha usually called her.

'What should we write in our story books, Miss Parpwell?' asked Sally Sweetpea, in a voice that sounded sicklier than jam tarts encased in candyfloss.

'What I want you to write, Sally,' replied Miss Parpwell, 'is a story about something that happened to you over the weekend. You have until lunchtime to finish it.'

Martha Mayhem knew exactly what her story was going to be about. She picked up her pencil immediately and began to write:

The Witch from the Ditch (with a twitch)

by Martha May(hem)

She chewed her pencil and decided to draw the witch, so her readers could picture who she was talking about.

'What's *that*?' asked Jack, looking up from his own story, which was about how Vicious Vlad (his hamster) had almost been sucked into the vacuum cleaner when he was let out of his cage while Jack practised his football skills. 'It looks like a peculiar pointy pet.'

'No, Jack, this is not a peculiar pointy pet,' Martha replied, forgetting she wasn't supposed to speak. 'This is the twitchy witch from the ditch I met this morning. She said I released a ghoul from the gate in Foxglove Field. That's what I meant was *scary*.

Not *hairy* – although the witch was pretty hairy. There were spiky bristles poking through her tights and four hairs on the end of her nose.'

'A hairy witch in a ditch? That's a good one, Martha.' Jack crumpled his forehead so it looked a lot like a crinkly crisp. 'Got it! What do you get if you cross a witch doing the washing-up with a ditch filled with dirty water?'

'Forget your joking for now, Jack,' Martha frowned. 'This is NOT the sort of thing you should joke about. This is SERIOUS.'

But Jack wasn't prepared to forget what he suspected might be one of his best jokes ever. 'It's dirty *witch*-water,' he explained. 'Like dirty *dish*water, but with a witch.'

Despite herself, a small smile slipped across Martha's lips, but the smile was so small that Jack began to wonder if this really *was* serious. 'Are you telling me that you *actually* saw a witch?'

'I am,' Martha nodded. 'And the witch told me that the ghoul from the gate might come after me. Jack, are you listening? An **ACTUAL GHOUL.**'

Jack was listening, all right. He was listening like he'd never listened before. He was listening so hard that Martha Mayhem's **EXTRAORDINARY** words clanged down his eardrums like enormous bells, just as a real bell went for lunch break.

The Storm in a Teacup

While Martha Mayhem was busy explaining the morning's **EXTRAORDINARY** events to Jack Joke, the witch from the ditch was busy with her own business . . .

After leaving Martha Mayhem in Foxglove Field, the witch from the ditch zoomed off down Lumpy Lane, puffing out her **ENORMOUS** purple polka-dot pants as she went. The wind billowed them out to a tremendous size and she rose

up,

up,

up

and away into the sky like a human hot-air balloon, proving that they weren't just a fashion accessory and they did, in fact, have an important function: they were **MAGICAL FLYING KNICKERS** (otherwise known as paranormal polka-dot pants).

'Argh-argh-ooo-yu-yu-eeeeeeeeeeeeeeee!'

went the witch as she landed on a prickly rose bush in Tacita Truelace's garden. 'Blithering bushes!' she cursed.

'Mee-aaahhhh-ooowwww!' yelped Trinket as the witch from the ditch trod on her tail.

'About time,' twitched the witch as Tacita Truelace rushed out of her tearoom to see what all the commotion was about. 'I need Helga-Holga. Where is she?'

'My word! If it isn't Griselda!' (Which was the witch's real name.) 'You're back sooner than I'd anticipated, but it's delightful to see you, sister.'

'I don't have time for niceties. There's an emergency,' sniffed Griselda Gritch (which was the witch's full name).

'What is it this time, Grizzie?' sighed Tacita Truelace. She had a feeling her sister's arrival was about to ruin her peaceful routine. After spending several decades working as a pilot and racing-car driver (following a brief spell as a Hollywood actress), Tacita Truelace was very happy with her quiet life in Cherry Hillsbottom. These days, her only excitement was taking Professor Gramps for a spin in her racing car on Sunday afternoons.

'I told you. There's an emergency,' said Griselda Gritch. 'Where's Helga-Holga? I've come to take her home to safety.'

Tacita Truelace chewed her bottom lip. 'There's a teensy-weensy problem with Helga-Holga. I think you'd better come inside. I shall close up the tearoom.'

She showed her sister inside and locked the door behind them.

'Tea with four sugars,' demanded Griselda Gritch, glancing at the menu.

Tacita Truelace's Tearoom
of Truly Tasty Treats

SAVOURY SENSATIONS
Professor's Pumpkin Pie
Cheery Cheesy Chutney Bap

SWEET SENSATIONS
Merry Martha Muffin
Jazzy Ginger Cake
Lovely Lemon Fizz Flan

SUNDAY'S SPECIAL SENSATION
Triple Cherry Chocolate Cake

'And a Merry Martha Muffin and a piece of Professor's Pumpkin Pie,' she added.

After serving her sister, Tacita Truelace poured herself a cup of tea to calm her nerves. She wasn't looking forward to revealing what the teensy-weensy problem was, mainly because her big sister was unlikely to agree that it *was* teensy-weensy.

'You needn't think feeding me all this food has made me forget why I'm here. WHERE is Helga-Holga?' demanded Griselda Gritch, picking pieces of pie crust from her chin.

Tacita Truelace patted her pink-lipsticked mouth with a flowery napkin and took a deep breath. 'I'm afraid she isn't here, Grizzie.'

'NOT HERE?' yelled Griselda, showering

the air with mushed-up muffin. 'You were supposed to look after her! I wouldn't have gone on my round-the-world witch-trip if you hadn't promised.'

'And she *is* being very well looked after. I wouldn't have left her with just anyone,' explained Tacita. 'The professor is an upstanding citizen, and a thoroughly charming chap.'

'Charming? Has your head gone gooey, sister? Stop blathering and get to the point!'

'It just didn't seem fair to keep her in my tiny garden. Helga-Holga needs space to run around, so my charming professor friend and his dear granddaughter have been taking care of her. They have the most delightful meadow.'

From the way Griselda was rapping her sharp knuckles on the table, Tacita sensed that her sister's impatience was about to reach new heights, so she thought better of describing the specific delights of the charming professor's meadow.

'We can visit her, of course, but first you must **CALM DOWN** and explain *exactly* what your emergency is, from the beginning.'

'If you insist,' grumbled Griselda Gritch. 'I wanted to surprise you and Helga-Holga for Halloween so I cut my trip short, but just as I approached Cherry Hillsbum –'

'I think you mean Hills*bottom*, dear!'

'All right, all right,' twitched Griselda Gritch. 'I was heading towards Cherry Hills*bottom* when this bothersome girl in a whirl sneezed an enormous sneeze and blasted a ghoul from a gate. Then the force of the ghoul gusting from the gate blew me into a ditch.'

'Slithering snakes!' gasped Tacita Truelace. 'Not a Gate Ghoul? Not the kind that never stops haunting?'

'Yes, *that* kind,' nodded Griselda Gritch gravely. 'One of *those*. I have no idea where it went, sister. Do you know any spells for finding and catching Gate Ghouls?'

'It's been so long,' sighed Tacita. 'I'm afraid the only spell I remember from my days at Madam Malenka's Academy of Enchantment is how to make people forget things.'

'That's no use at all,' growled Griselda Gritch. She slurped down the last of her tea. 'But I suppose I'll be all right, given that the girl released it, not me. Yikes and spikes! Look at the cup!' she squawked. 'These tea leaves foretell trouble, Tacita. *Tremendous* trouble. I see a storm brewing.'

'I'm sure it's nothing more than a storm

in a teacup,' Tacita comforted her. 'The ghoul might be a perfectly reasonable chap and go back into his gate of his own accord.'

'No, ninny, there's an ACTUAL storm in the teacup. Look!'

Griselda Gritch was right. There were storm clouds bubbling around the brim of the clattering cup, and the saucer was spinning like an **ACTUAL** flying saucer from outer space.

'Goodness to goshness! This *does* foretell trouble,' trembled Tacita Truelace, staring into the quivering cup. A few seconds later, once the storm clouds had dispersed, she noticed that the tea leaves had left a message. It read: Ditch Witch Whirl Girl Ghoul Get

'It seems to me that this Gate Ghoul is going to get you as well as the girl you mentioned!' gasped Tacita Truelace.

'ME?' shrieked the witch from the ditch, grabbing the teacup to see for herself. 'But the girl sneezed it out, not me.'

'From what I remember, ghouls aren't the sharpest of creatures. Maybe it saw the two of you near the gate and assumed you'd released it together,' Tacita suggested. 'Whatever the reason, it seems that the ghoul has plans for you both. We must search every nook and cranny of our brains until we remember how to deal with them. Let's shut ourselves in the basement and set up my spell apparatus.'

'But what about Helga-Holga?' grunted Griselda.

'We shall visit her later, Grizzie. She's perfectly safe.' Tacita took hold of her sister's bony hands and looked her in the eye. 'Unlike you.'

'Then what are we waiting for?' snapped Griselda. 'We've got spells to remember.'

7

A Disturbance of the *Peas*

While Griselda Gritch and Tacita Truelace were busy creating strange-smelling potions in the tearoom basement, Martha Mayhem and Jack Joke were queuing for lunch in the school canteen, which was also filled with strange smells.

'How many do you want, loveys? Two or three?' asked Mrs Gribble, the dinner lady, as she offered Martha and Jack a scoop of soggy fish fingers.

'None for me, thank you,' sighed Martha. The fish fingers reminded her of poor Elvis's floppy tail.

'You have to eat,' said Mrs Gribble. 'Always buzzing about, aren't you? You need plenty of food to keep up your strength.'

Considering it was only lunchtime and the day had already brought her several

'interesting challenges', as Professor Gramps might say, Martha thought Mrs Gribble had a point.

'In that case, please may I have four?' she asked. 'I *really* need to keep up my strength today.'

'Very well, lovey.' Mrs Gribble smiled. 'Mushy peas?'

'Yes, *peas*, Mrs Gribble,' said Jack, which was the joke he and Mrs Gribble shared whenever peas were on the menu. Even Jack had to admit this wasn't his funniest joke, but it always tickled Mrs Gribble, and he liked keeping his fans happy.

'What's up, Jack?' asked Mrs Gribble, slopping a spoonful of green mush onto his plate. 'You're not your usual jolly self today. You don't look very *pea*-sed to see me. In fact, you look pretty unhap-*pea*!'

'He's unhappy because I think a ghoul is going to get me, Mrs Gribble,' Martha explained. 'Do you happen to know anything about ghouls?'

'Dearie me!' chuckled Mrs Gribble, tucking a cloud of white hair under her hairnet. 'What imagination! And it's not even Halloween yet. Enjoy your lunch, loveys! I'd best get on serving everyone else. There's no peace for the wicked. Or should I say, no *peas* for the wicked!'

As they left the queue, Martha nudged Jack in the ribs. 'Do you think Mrs Gribble's hair looks suspicious?' she whispered.

'Suspicious?' Jack frowned. 'What do you mean?'

'You must have noticed Mrs Gribble touch her hair just then when I said the word "ghoul", and you must have noticed how her hair is all frizzy and silvery and looks a bit like a ghost, which is probably what a ghoul looks like. Maybe the ghoul followed me and thought Mrs Gribble's hair would be a good place to hide.

You know, to camouflage itself. Mrs Gribble could be in danger, Jack!'

'I'm not sure about that, Martha. I've never heard of ghouls haunting people's hair.'

'Neither have I, but there's always a first time. I need to consider all the evidence for and against Mrs Gribble's hair being haunted by a ghoul. That's what Professor Gramps would do.'

Martha closed her eyes so she could concentrate on all the evidence:

Reasons to think Mrs Gribble's hair is possessed by a ghoul:

1) Mrs Gribble's hair is frizzy and silvery and looks a bit ghostly (and ghosts are like ghouls).

Reasons to think Mrs Gribble's hair is _NOT_ possessed by a ghoul:

1) Mrs Gribble's hair hasn't tried to trick me by speaking in a sad-sounding voice.

2) Mrs Gribble's hair hasn't tried to haunt me (yet).

3) Jack and I have never heard of ghouls haunting people's hair.

Having carefully considered all the evidence, Martha came to the conclusion that Jack was probably right and Mrs Gribble's hair was NOT haunted by a ghoul. However, in the meantime, Jack had started to wonder if Martha might have a point. After what she'd experienced this morning, anything seemed possible, including a ghoul haunting a dinner lady's hair.

'Maybe we should check more closely,' he suggested. 'I mean, you can't see right *into* her hair from here.'

'Good thinking, Jack,' Martha agreed. 'We should investigate more thoroughly before ruling it out.'

Observing that Mrs Gribble was busy serving up plates of soggy fish fingers and mushy peas, Martha crept behind the counter and into the kitchen to find something to stand on. She spied a bucket and mop near the back door, both of which she thought would be useful tools for conducting her thorough investigation. She slinked back to the serving area, turned the bucket upside-down and stood on it. From this vantage point Martha had a much better view, and she noticed that Mrs Gribble's hairnet was covered in a dusty cobweb.

'Crumbs!' gasped Martha, thinking that there are few things more ghoulish than dusty cobwebs. With this extra point added to her list of 'Reasons to think Mrs Gribble's hair is possessed by a ghoul' she took a deep breath and extended the mop's handle towards Mrs Gribble, in order to lift up her hairnet to check for further evidence.

'Watch out!' Jack warned. 'The bucket is buckling!'

But it was already too late to prevent the **CANTEEN CATASTROPHE**. The bucket buckled and Martha fell to the floor, losing control of the mop as she landed. The handle knocked Sally Sweetpea's tray from her hands and in an instant Sally was transformed into a human island surrounded by a bright green ocean (mushy peas) and orange boats (fish fingers).

'What a clumsy clot!' yelled Sally Sweetpea, gesturing for the Sweetpea Sisters to come to her rescue (in case you're wondering, the Sweetpea Sisters were Sally's silly friends). 'And you can stop laughing, Sausage Fingers!' she shrieked at Jack.

'Uh-oh,' said Martha Mayhem. 'I'm sorry for making such a mess, Mrs Gribble. This wasn't supposed to happen. I was actually trying to save you from the gho. . .'

'What on EARTH has happened here?' interrupted Miss Parpwell, through lips that were even more turned down than usual (in fact, they were so turned down they were almost falling off her chin). 'And WHY on earth are you behind the serving area, Martha? Get out this instant and stop making such MAYHEM!'

'I was worried a ghoul was haunting Mrs Gribble's hair,' Martha explained. 'And while I was investigating, I saw a ghoulish cobweb on her hairnet. Look! It's right there!'

'Oh, lovey!' Mrs Gribble chuckled. 'Why didn't you just ask me? That must have come from the storeroom.' She removed the net, dusted off the cobweb and fluffed out her hair. 'No ghouls in here. Or should I say, no ghouls in *hair*! In fact, there are no ghouls any*hair*, because they don't exist. You and your imagination!'

'Indeed,' agreed Miss Parpwell. 'There are most definitely no such things as ghouls. Return to the classroom at once, Martha May. You can eat alone today. I am now *seriously* considering having *extremely* serious words with your grandfather.'

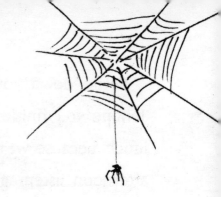

Telling Tales

Martha Mayhem cautiously crept back to the classroom, keeping a close eye out for the ghoul (and suspicious-looking hairstyles). But she arrived safely and, after finishing her food, decided to add some final touches to her drawing while she waited for lunch break to end. She'd just added a pointy hat to the witch's messy-haired head on the end of the witch's nose when the rest of the class returned to the room.

'Settle down,' ordered Miss Parpwell. 'I hope you finished your stories before lunch because we're going to spend this afternoon listening to them. Who would like to go first?'

Martha's hand shot into the air. She hadn't exactly finished *writing* her story, but her picture was ready and she thought she could just *tell* it. After all, encountering a witch in a ditch and unleashing a ghoul from a gate isn't the kind of thing

you forget. It was a long shot, but Martha also wondered if Miss Parpwell might even believe it was true if she heard the whole story.

'Please may I go first, Miss Parpwell?' asked Sally Sweetpea, who could see perfectly well that Martha had put her hand up first. She wasn't the kind of person who cared about things like that. *'Please?'*

'Don't you mean *peas*?' laughed Jack. 'You still have a load of them stuck to your skirt.'

'That's a good one!' laughed Nathaniel Hackett Crisp Packet, who was called Nathaniel Hackett Crisp Packet partly because it rhymed, and partly because he ate a lot of crisps, especially spaceship-shaped salt-and-vinegar-flavoured ones, which meant his dad, Horace Hackett the Grocer, had to order extra stock of them for his shop.

'Quiet!' called Miss Parpwell. 'Of course you may begin, Sally.'

'Thank you, Miss Parpwell.' Sally Sweetpea smiled, practically curtseying, as if Miss Parpwell were the Queen. She walked to the front of the class and began to read:

My Wonderful Weekend
By Sally Sweetpea

On Saturday morning, I went to my ballet class and my teacher told us the results of our exams. Because mine were so amazing, she said I might have to go to London to audition for the Royal Ballet School. After the class, Mummykins bought me a new pink princess costume as a reward. Then the Sweetpea Sisters came for tea and we ate fancy fairy cakes and pretended to be princesses with magical unicorns . . .

One by one, the class read out their stories. After Jack had made everyone laugh with his *True Tale of Vicious Vlad and the Va-va-vooming Vacuum Cleaner (or The Sucking Up of the Blood Sucker)*, Miss Parpwell tutted disapprovingly and checked her watch. 'Pack your things away,' she ordered.

'But, Miss Parpwell, what about me?' Martha protested, waving an arm in the air. It wasn't FAIR. She was the ONLY person who hadn't been allowed to tell her story.

'Very well, Martha, but be quick, and no nonsense.'

'The Witch from the Ditch,' Martha began, in the kind of hushed voice people use to tell tales of terror around campfires by the light of fat, creamy moons.

Today began VERY strangely when my pet Elvis wasn't his usual happy, hoggy self and I realised he was the one who'd made the mysterious muffled moaning noises I heard last night. But then things became EVEN stranger when I was on my way to school and heard a strange sad-sounding voice. Then I did an enormous sneeze that blasted a ghoul from the gate in Foxglove Field, and then I saw a VERY strange person who looked like a witch, because she ACTUALLY WAS a witch!

Martha held up her drawing.

'What on earth is THAT?' asked Miss Parpwell. 'I did NOT ask you to make up a Halloween story or draw pictures of witches. I asked you to write about something that actually happened.'

'But it *did* actually happen, Miss Parpwell. It's a *true* story. I tried to tell you when you found me in Trinket's cat flap, and that's why I was investigating Mrs Gribble's hair.'

'SIT DOWN!' shouted Miss Parpwell.

'But *please*, Miss Parp—'

'SIT DOWN! Or do you want to miss the Halloween party and spend every break time for a week in Mr Trumpton's office?'

Martha Mayhem sat down. She did not want to miss the Halloween party and spend every break time for a week in Mr Trumpton's office. She'd heard rumours that it stank of foul fishiness and rotten rats and mouldy mice because he did tons of trumps (he played the trumpet, so it had to be true). She scratched her legs. After all this bother, her tights were beginning to feel extra itchy.

'You're probably so itchy because you're

covered in horrid hog hair from that ugly creature you call a pet!' sneered Sally Sweetpea.

Before Martha had a chance to reply, the bell rang for the end of the day and the room was filled with the noise of chairs being scraped across the wooden floor and Miss Parpwell rapping a ruler on her desk.

'Don't forget to finish making your Halloween costumes this evening!' she shouted over the noise.

'I'm going to be a princess on a silver unicorn,' announced Sally Sweetpea.

'What do princesses have to do with Halloween?' laughed Jack.
'And unicorns aren't real.'

'I've wanted a unicorn for *ages*,' said Sally Sweetpea with a swoosh of her shiny hair. 'And I *always* get what I want.'

'I've had enough of this,' said Martha. 'Let's go, Jack. Jack? Are you listening?'

But Jack hadn't heard a word Martha had said. Jack was staring through the window in the direction of the football pitch, looking like he'd seen a ghost, which, as things were about to turn out, wasn't far from the truth . . .

9

The Mischievous Murky Mist

While Griselda Gritch was soaring down Lumpy Lane by the seat of her puffy pants to Tacita Truelace's Tearoom, and while Martha Mayhem was sprinting backwards down the lane after her, a murky mist was hovering over a tree near Paddlepong Pond, wondering what it was supposed to do . . .

The reason this murky mist was wondering what it was supposed to do was because it wasn't really a murky mist.

It just looked like one. It was actually the ghoul from the gate, and ghouls from gates aren't very good at remembering things.

What now? it wondered, thinking hard. And then it remembered. *Haunting! Haunt Ditch Witch and Whirl Girl!* Delighted that it had remembered what it was supposed to do, the ghoul floated towards the village, hoping to find the Whirl Girl or the Ditch Witch and feeling as light in spirit as it was in body. It wasn't long before it noticed a human being emerge from a pink building on Raspberry Road.

'Practise!' wheezed the ghoul. 'Practise haunting on human while watching for Whirl Girl and Ditch Witch!'

The ghoul whooshed down Raspberry

Road towards the human being, who happened to be Thelma from Thelma Tharton's Flower Emporium. She was on her way home from Peggy Pickle's Parlour, feeling very pleased with her fancy new hair-do, when a wild gust of wind whooshed around her.

'What a waste of money!' Thelma cried.
'My hair is ruined.' She scowled at the

murky grey mist hovering above
her head and waddled inside her
flower shop as fast as she could.

'Need more haunting happiness!' said
the murky grey mist (the ghoul), feeling
extremely excited to be back making
mischief after spending hundreds of years
imprisoned inside a gate. It drifted further
down Raspberry Road in search of someone
else to bother. As luck would have it (for
the ghoul), it spied Jack Joke's dad, Herbert

Sherbet the Butcher (it was less lucky for him), sweeping leaves from his doorway.

'Pretty pink things!' wheezed the ghoul as it noticed all the meat laid out inside the shop.

'Beefy botheration!' cursed Herbert Sherbet as a ghoulish gust blew the leaves all over the place. While he was busy sweeping them back up, the ghoulish gust seized the opportunity to slip inside the shop in search of some seriously meaty mischief.

'What the – ?' exclaimed Herbert, staggering backwards in shock as a string of sausages streamed from his shop and slithered towards him like a meaty snake. It slunk up his body and looped around his neck. 'What meaty madness is this?' he cried, struggling to loosen the sausagey scarf. 'I was saving them for the Halloween party.'

'Funny!' said the ghoul. 'Need more haunting fun.'

It glanced up Raspberry Road. It glanced down Raspberry Road. There didn't seem to be much going on in either direction, so it sailed upwards and rested on a branch. Within seconds it had dozed off and was dreaming of all the troublesome tricks it could play now it was free from being locked inside the gate.

A few hours later, the ghoul was woken by Trinket sharpening her claws on the tree trunk. *Where am I?* it wondered. *A-ha!*

it remembered. *Free from gate. Free for hauntings!* It sang a little song to remind itself of what it was supposed to do:

'A-haunting I shall go,
A-haunting I shall go,
Ditch Witch, Whirl girl,
A-haunting I shall go!'

The ghoul drifted down to the very end of Raspberry Road and noticed a building that was bigger than anything else it had seen in Cherry Hillsbottom. There was a sign outside the building that read:

Cherry Hillsbottom Village School

The ghoul soared *over* the gate, taking great care not to let any part of its vaporous body come into contact with it, just in case the Ghoul Guardians in charge of monitoring and managing ghoul behaviour had set a trap to reseal it inside the gate.

It floated around the back of the building and saw a patch of grass with white lines painted around its edges and poles at either end (the ghoul had forgotten about football pitches). As it went to investigate the netting behind the poles (it had also forgotten about goalposts), it noticed lots of small people sitting in rows inside the building. The ghoul watched as a bell clanged and the small people scraped back their chairs and stuffed things into bags. It drifted towards the building to get a better view. It was then that it caught the eye of a boy with hair like scrambled egg. And it was then that the boy with hair like scrambled egg noticed something. Something that looked a bit like a human-shaped mist. Something that made him look like he'd seen a ghost, which wasn't far from the truth . . .

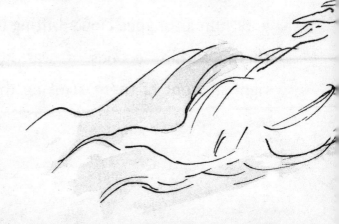

10

The Wispy Wind of Change

'M-M-M-Martha,' Jack jittered. 'Loooooook! It's the g-g-g-ghoul!'

Thinking Jack was probably playing a joke, Martha Mayhem went to the window expecting to see Mrs Gribble's hair. But this was no joke. This was the opposite of a joke. This was deadly serious. She could see a grey, human-shaped cloud drifting towards them. Within seconds, it was hovering right in front of them, stroking the glass with its wispy fingers as if it were tickling it. In the instant they saw one another, both Martha and the ghoul realised what they were looking at: this was the ghoul from the gate and she was the Whirl Girl.

'Uh-oh,' gasped Martha, twirling her twiggy plaits. 'We need a plan and we need it now!' She thought for a moment. 'Got it! Let's race to Tacita's Tearoom. The witch from the ditch might be there.'

'M-m-m-maybe we should stay here until it l-l-l-leaves,' Jack jabbered.

'Professor Gramps says it's better to face your fears, not flee from them, and he knows about things like that.' Martha went to the door. 'We'll leave on the count of five, OK? One, two, three, four . . .'

'No! I . . . um . . . I just remembered I'm supposed to be at football practice.'

Martha Mayhem crinkled her brow. 'That's not today.' Then, realising Jack had only said this because he didn't want to admit how scared he was, she knew just what to say. 'I can't go out there on my own, Jack. I need you with me. We should stick together. You know, like when you're marking someone in a match.'

'All right,' Jack nodded. He was still jittering with dread, but couldn't let Martha do this alone. 'If you need me.'

Arm in arm, Martha and Jack raced up Raspberry Road. As they reached Thelma Tharton's Flower Emporium, the wispy, grey, human-shaped cloud swooped down

in front of them and took a great gulp
of air. It swelled to the size of a tent and
wheezed a windy rhyme:

'A-haunting I shall go,
A-haunting I shall go,
Ditch Witch, Whirl Girl,
A-haunting I shall go!'

It puffed Martha Mayhem and Jack Joke
right *past* Tacita's Tearoom and all the way
up Lumpy Lane. As they hurtled by Foxglove
Field, Martha could feel its ghostly breath
on her neck. It felt colder than anything
she'd ever known — even colder than the
time she'd done an experiment to see how

103

many ice lollies she could eat in one sitting (it was twelve, in case you're wondering, and made Martha so cold that she didn't stop shivering for several hours).

'Faster, Jack, faster,' panted Martha, secretly wondering how much longer she'd be able to keep running. But she wasn't the only one feeling exhausted by all this

activity. The ghoul was also in serious need of a rest (imagine how tired you'd feel if you were an ancient ghoul who'd been locked inside a gate and this was your first haunting for hundreds of years) and decided to take a break, but not before making sure Martha Mayhem knew it had plans for her.

'A-haunting's what I do,
A-haunting's what I do,
Hurly-burly girly whirly
I'll be back for you!'

. . . it wheezed before floating away in search of somewhere to snooze.

Feeling as relieved as you might do after going to the loo following a long, bumpy car journey during which you'd drunk ten bottles of juice, Martha Mayhem and Jack Joke slowed to a jog. They'd just about caught their breath as they neared Martha's house at the end of the lane.

'Thank goodness it's gone. At least, gone

for now, and we can tell Gramps all about it. He'll believe me. He'll help us. I wonder if he managed to work out what's wrong with Elvis . . . Gramps, we're home!'

But the house was dark, and there was no sign of Professor Gramps.

'I expect he's working in his library,' suggested Martha, trying her hardest not to worry.

But the library was also dark. Martha switched on the light. There was no sign of Professor Gramps there either, which made it impossible not to worry.

'Are you thinking what I'm thinking?' asked Jack.

Martha scratched her toilet-roll tights. 'I *think* I probably am,' she confessed. 'Are you thinking that Professor Gramps might have been ... might have been ... *ghoul-napped*?' Her lower lip quivered, her shoulders shuddered and a tiny tear trickled down her cheek. 'He probably spent the ENTIRE day doing research about hogs for me and all I've done is get him *ghoul-napped*.'

'Shall we hide under the desk until he comes h-h-h-home?' asked Jack, who was now jittering like never before.

Martha twirled her twiggy plaits thoughtfully. 'I don't think hiding would help, Jack. We need to launch an investigation. We'll start by conducting a thorough search of the area. You know, for clues.'

She shuffled through the muddle on Professor Gramps's desk and found some sheets of paper covered in his scrawly scribblings.

'Just as I thought!' cried Martha. 'Look, here's a clue! Gramps's scribblings bring me to the conclusion that he went missing several hours after I went to school.'

'Eh?' Jack looked baffled.

'He had time to do all this research before he was ghoul-napped,' Martha explained. She read the research aloud:

ELVIS'S SYMPTOMS:

a) Making peculiar moaning noises

b) Droopiness

Diagnosis:

In this particular instance, Elvis probably has a case of Lonely-itis. The peculiar noises could be a call to the thing/animal/person he is missing.

Treatment:

a) Reunite him with the thing/animal/person he is missing

b) Give him extra treats (for example, extra fruity roots) to take his mind off his loneliness

'Excellent!' Martha exclaimed. 'So we know what's wrong with Elvis and how to make him better, and we also know that Gramps can't have been gone all day, but that's not enough.' She thought for a moment. 'I need to check on Elvis RIGHT AWAY. I wonder who he's missing. I suppose it might be Miss Truelace, but he sees her practically every day.'

As she went to the door, Martha heard an odd puffing noise just the other side of it, like the sound of a balloon being deflated. This was followed by an angry knocking on the door itself.

'Uh-oh,' said Martha. 'Hold tight, Jack. I think we're in for a rocky ride.'

II

A Revelatory Reunion

Martha Mayhem took a deep breath and opened the door.

'Oh,' said Griselda Gritch, with a twitch. 'It's *you*.'

'And it's *you*!' exclaimed Martha Mayhem, who had no trouble recognising the witch from the ditch beneath her disguise. Tacita Truelace, who was standing beside the witch, had convinced her sister to conceal her clothes so as not to alarm the villagers of Cherry Hillsbottom, who weren't at all used to seeing witches. Although, it has to be said, the disguise hardly helped her blend in. She was wearing an eggy-yellow mac covered in bright blue dots, a curly blonde wig and a huge pair of sunglasses.

'I was hoping to see you again,' said Martha Mayhem. She turned to Jack. 'This is the witch from the ditch,' she explained, although he'd already worked that out. Her stripy tights were peeping out from the mac, and there was no missing the four bristly hairs on the end of her nose.

'Why have you brought me here, sister? *This* is the bothersome girl in a whirl,' snapped the witch from the ditch to

Tacita. 'She's to blame for the incident with the ghoul from the gate.'

'Oi! Don't blame Martha!' said Jack, jumping to her defence.

'Please, there's no time for arguing,' said Martha. 'I think Gramps has been ghoul-napped, and maybe Elvis too. We were about to check on him when you arrived.'

'Giddy gooseberries!' moaned Tacita Truelace. 'Not the charming professor! Not by that ghastly ghoul! And maybe Elvis too, you say?' She glanced at Griselda Gritch. 'We haven't seen the ghoul all day, so I'd rather hoped it had drifted off somewhere else.'

'I'm afraid it hasn't gone anywhere, Miss Truelace. It chased us home from school. What are we going to do?'

'Piff, paff, poof!' scoffed Griselda Gritch. 'Here's what I'm going to do:

LEAVE THIS LOUSY VILLAGE!

All I care about is Helga-Holga. You said she was here, sister. You *promised* she was here. So **WHERE IS SHE?** As soon as I find her, I'm taking her home to my creepy castle.'

Just then, a monstrous moan erupted. It sounded a bit like this:

Aaquwwwww – oooooh –
aaahhhooo ww!

'Helga-Holga!' hollered Griselda Gritch. 'Where are you, my darling?'

'What *are* you talking about?' Martha frowned. 'That's Elvis, my handsome hog. It sounds like Gramps didn't have a chance to treat him, but thank goodness he hasn't gone missing too.'

'Little humans are supposed to have dogs, not hogs. And you're wrong. *Her* name is Helga-Holga and she's most definitely MINE.'

'Is that true, Miss Truelace?' asked Martha. Could her adorable Elvis *really* belong to grumpy Griselda? And what if she really wanted to take him away? At that thought, Martha's heart fluttered like a little bird.

Tacita Truelace chewed her lower lip. 'It is, Miss Martha. Before she came to stay with you, and before she came to me, Elvis was named Helga-Holga and my sister looked after her. Grizzie left her with me while she went off on a round-the-world trip.'

'Oh, I hadn't realised he might have to leave.' Martha suddenly felt as sad as Elvis had looked after breakfast this morning. What if she *never* saw Elvis ever again? But then An Illuminating Thought zonked her on the bonce.

'Yikes!' yelled Martha. She looked from Tacita to Griselda with big boggly eyes and started to shake all over. If she'd been a milkshake, she would have been the frothiest milkshake in the entire universe. 'So *that's* why he wasn't himself this morning. Gramps's research was right! Elvis DOES have Lonely-itis. He . . . I mean, *she*, must have been missing you. Of *course* you can visit him – I mean, her – and then we'll all look for Gramps. Follow me!'

As they neared the pen, Helga-Holga unfurled herself. As soon as she caught sight of Griselda Gritch, her tail sprang back to its usual perky state.

'I'm so happy to see you back to normal!' cried Martha, grinning the grinniest grin she'd ever grinned. It was as if she'd won the Kingdom of Grindom's Annual Grinning Contest.

Griselda Gritch leapt into the pen and threw her arms around Helga-Holga's neck. The happy, hairy hog nuzzled against Griselda's knees, making a satisfied snuffling sound.

'I have some jewels for you, from my travels!' remembered the witch. After some rummaging around in the pockets of her pants, Griselda fastened a diamond collar around Helga-Holga's neck and clipped a bejewelled bracelet around each of her legs.

'It's simply marvellous to see Helga-Holga so happy,' enthused Tacita Truelace. 'In fact, it's rather touching.' She paused to dab her eyes. 'But there are still a number of serious matters to be resolved, namely the matter of the dear professor being missing, and the matter of locating the escaped Gate Ghoul, not to mention the matter of ascertaining whether the aforementioned matters are connected.'

While he wasn't sure what all these tricky words meant, Jack was pretty sure that he'd come up with a smart solution to all the serious matters. 'If you *are* really witches, can't you just do a spell to find Gramps? And one to get rid of the ghoul?'

Tacita Truelace shook her head sadly. 'We've spent all day experimenting with spells, but none of them can have worked if the ghoul is still among us. The only spell I can remember properly is how to make people forget things.'

'Are you *sure* you're *really* witches?' asked Jack.

'How **DARE** you . . . ?' twitched Griselda Gritch.

Tacita Truelace silenced her sister with a splinter-sharp stare. 'As Martha said, this is no time for arguing. This is time for working together to find Professor Gramps.' She turned to Jack. 'Yes, we really are both witches. I know I don't look like a conventional one, but I've never been one to conform. Talking of nonconformity,' she added with a smile, 'I know exactly how we should search for the professor. Grizzie, fire up your flying machine!'

'Flying machine?' spluttered Martha Mayhem.

'I'll give you flying machine!' grumbled Griselda Gritch. All she wanted to do was return home to her creepy castle, but when Helga-Holga gently tugged on the bottom of her bloomers, as if expressing agreement with Tacita's suggestion, Griselda was forced to change her mind. She found it impossible to refuse Helga-Holga anything.

'Very well,' huffed the witch from the ditch. 'But you needn't think we're staying in this troublesome town for long. Vlad will be missing us. Vlad is our vampire butler,' she clarified boastfully.

Jack's ears pricked up. He wondered if this vampire butler might be related to his hamster, but he soon forgot about that when he saw the witch from the ditch puff out her ENORMOUS puffy purple polka-dot pants. Once they were at maximum capacity, Tacita Truelace and Helga-Holga jumped inside.

'So *that's* why you don't need a broomstick!' marvelled Martha Mayhem. 'You have MAGICAL FLYING KNICKERS!'

'Are they powered by . . . you know . . . by bottom air?! Are they PARPY PANTS?' spluttered Jack. 'I bet Miss *Parp*well would love a pair of those! Do you have any TRUMPING TROUSERS that Mr Trumpton could borrow?'

'They have *nothing* to do with bottom air, Master Jack,' explained Tacita Truelace. 'They are NOT Parpy Pants. I suppose they are better described as Balloon Bloomers. Now jump in, there's no time to waste.'

'What if they tear?' Jack fretted. 'What if we tumble out?'

'Stop worrying, Jack. I need you. I'm *so* worried about Gramps. And don't you remember what I said about fighting your fears?' begged Martha desperately, all the while observing that the perilous-looking pants were now hovering a few feet off the ground. They'd have to make a jump for it, and fast, before the bloomers drifted too high. She took hold

of Jack's hand. 'One, two, three . . .' she
counted, and together they leapt into the
pants.

Unfortunately, Martha leapt with too much force and the enormous knickers slipped down Griselda's skinny legs, taking the passengers with them. They all toppled onto Professor Gramps's rock garden.

'Didn't I say we were in for a rocky ride?' Martha laughed.

Jack didn't find it at all funny, and neither did Griselda Gritch. Jack was covered in mud and trembling with terror, while the witch was stripped down to her stripy tights, trembling with rage at the Whirl Girl, who'd caused her nothing but bother since the moment they'd met.

'Hurry and sort yourself out, sister,' insisted Tacita Truelace. 'We must locate the charming professor!'

Grumpily, Griselda Gritch pulled up her puffy pants. Everyone climbed back inside and they bobbed up, up and away into the cold, black sky.

12

The Hump in the Hedge

The ENORMOUS puffy purple polka-dot pants and their passengers rose precariously into the night. The air was frosty, the moon was as full and fat as a doughy roll, and the pants were a mixing pot of many feelings – Jack's jitteriness, Tacita Truelace's trepidation, Griselda Gritch's grouchiness, Helga-Holga's hogginess and Martha Mayhem's mega-massive need to rescue her gramps from the grip of the ghoul.

They soared along Lumpy Lane and over Foxglove Field, focused on their mission, but as they floated beyond Paddlepong Pond, Griselda Gritch started to twitch. 'This is like looking for a particular grain of sand along the world's longest beach,' she complained. 'Wholly hopeless.'

'Shame on you, sister,' tutted Tacita Truelace. 'We're not giving up. The darling professor needs us!'

While the witch sisters squabbled, Martha Mayhem cupped her hands around her ears, trying to block out their bickering. 'Shh!!' she hissed. 'I can hear something.' She listened hard. There it was again: an unmistakable mumbling coming from somewhere beneath them.

'The capital of Tahiti is Papeete. The national bird of Dominica is the Sisserou parrot . . .'

'That's Gramps!' said Martha, her heart beating with excitement. 'He must be close!'

'Eh?' said Griselda Gritch. 'Are you always so full of nonsense?'

'It's not nonsense. I'm using my powers of deduction,' Martha explained. 'Gramps mumbles fascinating facts in his sleep, so I deduce that he has to be somewhere nearby. Please could you hover a little lower so I can have a closer look?'

'I'm NOT your private chauffeur,' snapped Griselda Gritch.

'Seeing as it's imperative that we follow any leads, it would be most appreciated if you *could* navigate us a little lower,' said Tacita Truelace, and Helga-Holga expressed her agreement by releasing a series of serious-sounding snorts. Having little choice, Griselda Gritch patted the pants to deflate them a little and they dropped a few feet closer to the ground.

'The Bribri people are indigenous to Costa Rica. The blue-ringed octopus has enough venom to poison twenty-six humans . . .'

went the unmistakeable mumbling.

And then Martha saw the source of the mumbling – a hump in a hedge wearing a woolly mustard suit.

'Grrr-aaaaaaa-mmmp-sssss!' she cried, jumping out of the pants. She landed with a thud and whizzed towards him. 'Are you all right?' she asked, laying a hand on his forehead. 'Were you ghoul-napped?'

Professor Gramps opened his owl-like eyes and saw a pair of ENORMOUS puffy purple polka-dot pants hovering overhead and Martha Mayhem's heart-shaped face looking down at him.

'Ghoul-napped? I don't know about that,' said Professor Gramps.

He rubbed his eyes, hoping to erase the extremely strange sight of Griselda's ENORMOUS flying knickers, which had just landed a short distance away. 'But I do know that I must still be dreaming. What other explanation is there for me seeing Miss Truelace tangled up in a pair of billowing bloomers with a wonky-wigged woman?'

'This isn't a dream, Gramps,' said Martha seriously. 'It's extremely real.'

After Martha had told him all the EXTRAORDINARY events that had happened that day, Professor Gramps cracked his knuckles and pulled himself to his feet. 'Hmm,' he remarked thoughtfully. 'I've never heard – or seen – anything like it. Are you sure we're not *both* dreaming?'

'It's all true, dear professor,' said Tacita Truelace, smoothing down her dress, for their landing had been anything but

 smooth. 'Every last word.'

'Heebie-ba-jeebies!' exploded Professor Gramps. 'Tickle me with a feather, Tacita!

So you really are a witch?' He looked from Tacita to Griselda, and then to Martha, who were all nodding their heads. 'Hoo-hoo!' he hooted. 'In all my years of study I have never encountered real witches. I'm surprised you kept it from me, Tacita. And Martha, I'm sorry I doubted you. The first rule of being a good researcher, not to mention being your granddad, is to keep an open mind.'

'That's OK, Gramps, I'm just glad we found you. But why were you heaped in this hedge? *Was* it the ghoul?'

'I was on my way home from Plumtum Town — I'd gone there to find some tasty treats for Elvis — when a great gust of wind blew me here. I became caught up in the brambles, and all the effort of untangling myself must have worn me out. As you know, I don't usually fall asleep in hedges.'

'Perhaps that great gust was actually the ghoul, Professor Gramps,' suggested Jack. 'It blew us all the way home from school.'

'That's an interesting thought, Jack,' mused Professor Gramps. 'It may well have been the ghoul. It was an unusually great gust, and accompanied by peculiar, sad-sounding wails. I assumed it was the wind whistling in my eardrums.'

'That sounds exactly like the ghoul! We need to do something about it as **SOON** as possible,' said Martha. 'Research?' she suggested, raising an eyebrow at Professor Gramps.

'Took the words right out of my mouth,' he replied, before turning to Griselda Gritch. 'Would you be so kind as to give us a lift home in your most remarkable flying machine?'

Even grumpy Griselda couldn't resist Professor Gramps's charming manners, so she puffed out her purple polka-dot pants and they sailed back home to Cherry Hillsbottom.

13

In which Martha Mayhem Displays Spook-tacular Study Skills

After settling Helga-Holga in her pen for the night, with a bed of fresh straw and plenty of fruity roots, Griselda Gritch prepared her ENORMOUS purple polka-dot pants for yet another flight.

'I advise you to make as little fuss as possible when you take Jack home,' warned Professor Gramps. 'I am of the opinion that this is a matter we should keep to ourselves. I suspect the villagers of Cherry Hillsbottom will find it tricky to believe our story.'

'I completely agree,' said Jack. 'I reckon you should drop me right at the end of my garden, or even next door. Mum and Dad would have a fit if they saw me zooming around in these pants! See you tomorrow, Martha, and good luck with the research.'

'Thanks, Jack,' Martha called as he began to rise. 'Hold on tight!' Once Jack, Tacita and Griselda had vanished into the big, black sky, she took hold of Gramps's hand. 'Shall we go to the library now?'

'A marvellous plan, my Fabulous Fact Fiend,' said Professor Gramps.

Inside the library shed, Martha Mayhem went through Gramps's books, which were arranged alphabetically, from *Aardvarks in*

Antiquity to *Zany Zoology*. She found the 'G' section.

'*Gardening in Ghana . . . The Geography of Giants . . . Ghost Gangs of Grinstead . . . Ghouls: An Extremely Extensive Introduction* — here we go!'

'That was a graduation gift from the Fellow of Phantoms at my university,' said Professor Gramps. 'I never imagined I'd need it to solve a *practical* problem.'

Martha began to read out loud.

CHAPTER ONE

Introductory Facts about Ghouls

- Ghouls look a lot like murky grey mist, which means human beings often mistake them for murky grey mist.

- Ghouls love playing silly tricks on human beings, and can be remarkably quick-fingered.

- Ghouls have terrible memories and often forget what they're doing while they're actually doing it.

- Ghouls are very keen on fairies and princesses. In fact, contrary to common belief, they are attracted to all kinds of shiny things, sparkly things and pink things.

- Ghouls are immune to all known spells. That is to say, no known spells work on ghouls.

'Then there's no point in Miss Truelace and the witch from the ditch trying to remember spells,' sighed Martha. She read on.

CHAPTER TWO

Ghouls from Gates and the Role of Ghoul Guardians

- Ghoul Guardians are a kind of ghoul police force, an organisation that decides if naughty ghouls should be locked away in gates.

- Ghoul Guardians may decide to lock naughty ghouls inside gates (or fences) as punishment for committing too many silly hauntings, and for giving ghouls a reputation for being foolish.

- Ghouls from gates sometimes try to trick people into releasing them by making sad wailing sounds.

- Once released, they will cause trouble for the person who released them for ever. Several cases have been reported of ghouls causing trouble for associates of the person who released them, also for ever.

'For ever?!' gasped Martha Mayhem.

'Don't panic,' said Professor Gramps. 'Read this next section.'

'Most interesting,' said Professor Gramps.

Guidance for Victims of Gate Ghoul Hauntings:

- A person being haunted by a Gate Ghoul could try to trick it into haunting another human being, but it should be noted that Gate Ghouls can only be tricked into haunting things they like.

- Alternatively, a human being haunted by a Gate Ghoul could try to puff it back inside the gate, although reports of this method being successfully implemented are scarce.

'Plenty to oil our brain cogs there. Why don't we get a breath of fresh air to clear our minds? Look, the sun is already rising. We've worked through the night!'

As they trooped out to the meadow and the sun glinted on Helga-Holga's diamond collar, Martha Mayhem felt the force of **An Incredible Idea** rise from her toes and pop out through her nose in the form of an(other) **ALMIGHTY SNEEZE**.

The blast blew Professor Gramps backwards into his wheelbarrow, the sight of which sent Martha Mayhem's mind a-spinning with **A Second Sensational Idea.**

'I think I might have come up with a plan to get rid of the ghoul from the gate!' she cried.

Professor Gramps heaved himself out of the barrow. 'What did I tell you about fresh air clearing the mind?' He beamed. 'That's superb. Let's discuss it over a celebratory breakfast of scrambled eggs and chocolate milk, with a side helping of gingery jam on crumpets.'

The Rowdy Rumpus
on Raspberry Road

With her belly full of breakfast and her brain bursting with plans, Martha skipped to school, making a list of all the things she needed to do during the day as she went.

List of things I need to do today:

- Go to school

- Finish preparing The Plan

- Go to the annual Cherry Hillsbottom Halloween party

- Get the ghoul from the gate back into the gate

Unfortunately, while Martha was going over her plan to put everything right, everything around her started to go spectacularly *wrong* . . .

The wrongness began when a great, grey gust of wind (the ghoul) swelled up behind her as she approached Peggy Pickle's Parlour. The gust was so great that Martha had to grab hold of the nearest cherry tree to stay upright. While she was gripping the trunk with all her might, with her curly-whirly hair blowing up and out in all directions, Martha felt the wind whoosh past her towards the salon door. She released her grip and rushed inside, hoping with all her heart that the ghoul wasn't making too much mischief.

'CRIPES!' cried Martha. Through a fog of hairspray, she spied a scene of considerable chaos. There were shampoo squirts on the ceiling, brushes in the basins and hair clippings all over the floor. Martha's toilet-roll tights started to tingle like never before, no doubt due to the fact that she sensed trouble was ahead. And indeed it was, in the form of an extremely angry-

looking Miss Pickle. She'd emerged from the backroom of the parlour, still wearing her dressing gown, with her face covered in thick green slime, which Martha supposed must be some kind of cream designed to make her face look nice (although it has to be said that, at this precise moment, Peggy Pickle looked more like a swamp monster than someone with a nice face).

'What's all this?' spluttered Peggy through the haze of hairspray. 'Have I been broken into, or are *you* responsible for making all this mayhem, Martha May? If you ARE responsible, your granddad will be VERY disappointed in you.'

Very aware that the trouble was no longer ahead (it was, in fact, RIGHT in front of her), Martha tried to think of a way to explain all this without mentioning ghouls or witches. But her thoughts were interrupted by a high-pitched screech.

It was such a sharp sound, Martha was certain it could have cut the world's toughest diamond into several shards.

'What's THIS?' Peggy was pointing at one of her mirrors. A rather rude message had been sprayed onto it with hair lotion:

Peggy Pickle's Poopy Parlour

And to make things worse, there were three big kisses at the end of the message.

X X X

'It *WAS* you, wasn't it? Well, blow me down!'

'Uh-oh,' said Martha. 'That's possibly the worst thing you could have said, Miss Pickle.' And Martha was right.

Taking Peggy Pickle's words literally, the ghoul created a fresh flurry of wind. It whirled around Peggy and she began to spin and spin like she was trapped inside a tornado. While Martha grabbed hold of a chair to stop herself from spinning, the harried hairdresser became so dizzy that she was, in fact, blown down. But matters didn't end there. One final wind blast blew the hair clippings up from the floor. Most of them landed on Miss Pickle and stuck to her slimy face cream, giving her the appearance of someone who'd grown a bushy beard over their ENTIRE face.

Even though this was an extremely silly sight, laughing was the last thing on Martha's mind. She had to do *something* before things got even more out of hand. She glanced around the salon for inspiration. 'Got it!' She grabbed a hairdryer and blasted it, hoping the warm air would gust the ghoul from the room once and for all. After a few moments, Martha managed to steer the ghoul towards the door, and with one final close-range blast the ghoul left (along with the hair clippings that hadn't fixed themselves to Miss Pickle's face).

'It's all sorted now, Miss Pickle.' Martha breathed a sigh of relief.

'Sorted? *Sorted?!* Look at the state of this

place. And look at the state of ME!' howled Peggy, catching sight of herself in the mirror through the rather rude message. 'Why on earth did you do this to my parlour, Martha? And to my *face*? And *how*?'

'It wasn't me, Miss Pickle. The wind just sort of whirled you around and blew the hair onto you.'

'That's one of the most unbelievable stories I've ever heard. I don't know *how*, but I'm pretty sure this *IS* all your fault. Now shoo, before you do any further damage!'

Feeling like a saggy balloon, Martha left the salon, stepping over the stray hair clippings and keeping an eye out for any grey gusts. She trudged down Raspberry

Road, wondering how much trouble she was going to get in for something that really wasn't all her fault. 'I just want to put everything right,' she sighed. 'I want all this wrongness to stop.'

Unfortunately it's not always possible to get what you want, and on this occasion Martha got the exact opposite of what she wanted. That is to say, rather than stopping, the wrongness started up all over again when another great grey gust of wind (the ghoul) whooshed down the road. Within seconds, a new bout of bedlam began, this time outside Thelma Tharton's Flower Emporium, where dozens of flowerpot displays were thrown to the ground.

By the time Martha reached the scene, the pavement was covered in soil and bits of broken pots. Furthermore, the ghoul was now pulling every single petal from every single flower.

'Stop that right now!' Martha ordered, not imagining for one moment

that the ghoul would pay any attention to her. So you can imagine her surprise when the ghoul actually did stop. Martha was even more surprised when its vaporous hands picked up each pretty pink petal and started to arrange them into a neat pattern across Mrs Tharton's doorstep.

It was almost as if it was tidying up the mess it had made!

'I didn't think ghouls would like flower arranging, but it just goes to show that you shouldn't make assumptions.' Martha smiled in relief. 'I'm glad you're making an effort to tidy things up.'

Just then, Martha felt a wide shadow loom over her.

'What's happened here?' asked Thelma Tharton the florist, her plump pink face frowning in a mix of bafflement and anger.

'It's pretty gusty today,' Martha explained. 'I'm afraid an especially big gust seems to have blown over your pots.'

'There's no gust now,' observed Mrs Tharton, her eyes narrowing into a suspicious glare.

'Well, it was definitely gusty a few moments ago. I'll help clear this up, if you like,' Martha offered. 'It's not *that* bad,' she added, noticing that Mrs Tharton's nostrils had widened to at least three times their usual width, and her increasingly angry-looking face was now the colour of strawberry ice cream.

'Not that bad? Not that *BAD*?' Mrs Tharton raged. 'My best flowerpots have been smashed to smithereens, there's soil ALL OVER the pavement and SOMEONE has made a rude arrangement with MY petals!'

'Rude? What do you mean, Mrs – Cripes!' Martha interrupted herself when she saw EXACTLY what Thelma Tharton meant. The ghoul had indeed tidied up the petals, but unfortunately it had arranged them into a rude message.

If you're wondering, the message read

'Poopy Pongy Petals'.

'It wasn't me, Mrs Tharton. It really wasn't. I'll clear everything up though.'

'Then who was it, Martha?' The florist's cheeks were now the colour of raspberry sauce. 'These flowers were in their pots a minute ago, with their petals firmly attached. *Someone* must have done it, and there's no one here but you, so that *someone* has to be you. I'll have to have a word with your grandfather about you making all this mayhem.'

Thelma Tharton had barely stopped speaking before Martha sensed a chilly presence.

'Duck!' Martha cried. 'Your pinkness is putting you in PERIL!'

Martha was right. Having taken a fancy to the increasing pinkness of Thelma's face (all ghouls like pink), the ghoul was speeding towards her. Martha leapt forwards, hoping to put herself between the flustered florist and the ghoul.

But she lunged too hard and sent Mrs Tharton flying backwards into the shop, right into her miniature pond and water feature. After some splashing and spluttering, Thelma emerged with a pile of lily pads on her head, pond fronds in her hair and a furious expression on her now scarlet face.

'Are you all right, Mrs Tharton?' Martha gasped. 'I didn't mean for this to happen. I was trying to protect you.'

'Protect me? *Protect* me?! You half drowned me! You've made me look like a right fool! I'm soaked through.'

'Oh, you don't look like a fool, Mrs Tharton. You look more like a moody mermaid with seaweed for hair and a hat made from a stack of green pancakes.' (It was true – the pile of lily pads *did* look remarkably like a stack of shiny green pancakes.)

'A moody mermaid? *Pancake* hat?' Mrs Tharton flipped the lily pads from her head in fury. 'I feel quite sorry for your grandfather, having such a menace to deal with. Be off with you!'

Feeling like an utterly deflated balloon, Martha left Thelma Tharton flipping her pond pancakes and started walking down Raspberry Road. She was pretty sure Professor Gramps would *never* think of her as a menace, but she simply had to put a stop to the ghoul before the entire village came to think of her as one.

But where is it now? Martha wondered as she stepped over the rude arrangement of petals and piles of soil.

'No way!' Martha couldn't believe her eyes. She'd just seen *exactly* where the ghoul was. Or, to be more precise, where it had been. While there was no sign of the ghoul itself, there *was* a sign that it had already paid a visit to Nanny Nuckey's Knitting Shop, just a little further down the road. In fact, there was an *actual* sign in the form of a brand-new woolly banner that had been strung up between two cherry trees. The sign had been woven from several balls of wool and the words

Nanny Nuckey wears knitted knickers

were on FULL SHOW right across Raspberry Road. (If there are any parents or teachers reading this, there weren't any ACTUAL knitted knickers on show.) As Martha began to assess whether she'd be able to climb the trees to remove the message before dear old Nanny Nuckey saw it, a soft sound grabbed her attention.

'Help me!' said a quiet, quivery voice.

Martha whipped round, expecting it to be the ghoul disguising its voice again, but instead she saw something white and fluffy in the window of the knitting shop, and this something looked a lot like a colossal caterpillar cocoon.

'Is that you, Martha?' came the quivery cocoon voice. 'My eyes aren't what they used to be.'

Martha tingled with shock. Was that a

talking cocoon? A talking cocoon that knew her name? Making a mental note to ask her mum and dad about this extraordinary

phenomenon (being Professors of Creeping Creatures, they'd surely know *exactly* what it was), Martha cautiously edged towards the window and noticed something extra odd about the cocoon-like object. It was made of wool, and there was a small, silvery dome poking from its top.

'Nanny Nuckey!' Martha cried. Up close, she could see that the small silvery dome was, in fact, the old lady's hair bun. 'For a moment I thought you were a talking caterpillar! Don't worry, I'll soon unravel you,' Martha promised. 'You've gone too far this time!' she yelled into the sky, before rushing to Nanny Nuckey's rescue. She was the oldest resident in the entire village, older even than Professor Gramps. She was so old, she'd lost track of when she was born, although Gramps was certain he could recall a street party to celebrate her 100th birthday back in the early 1990s.

'Oh, Martha! I can't thank you enough,' said Nanny Nuckey as Martha unwound her from the wool. 'Now, quick, close the door! It seems that Cherry Hillsbottom is in the throes of a hurricane! I've never felt such wind. It burst into the shop and somehow unravelled every ball of wool and wrapped it around me.

Goodness knows what's going on. That nice young man who does the weather reports didn't forecast a hurricane. I feel quite giddy.'

'I don't think anyone could have forecast this, Nanny Nuckey,' said Martha. 'Is there anything I can do to help your giddiness?'

'I'll be right as rain once I've had my cup of tea. Be a dear and fetch it for me, won't you? I left it over on the counter.'

'Of course!' While Martha was glad that Nanny Nuckey seemed to be recovering, she was far from glad that the ghoul had done such a thing to such an old lady in the first place. 'Here it is.'

Nanny Nuckey drank down the tea and smacked her lips. 'Thank you, Martha. I feel much better now. I should give you a reward for rescuing me. Goodness knows what I'd have done if you hadn't come along.'

'I'm just glad you're feeling better. I really don't need a reward,' said Martha, thinking to herself that a reward was the *last* thing she deserved, seeing as she was the reason the ghoul had escaped.

'Reward? **REWARD?!** This menace-maker certainly doesn't need a reward!' Peggy Pickle hollered from the doorway. While she'd wiped off most of the face cream, Martha noticed that she'd forgotten the area around her lips, so it looked like she had a skinny multicoloured moustache.

'You're a disgrace, Martha May!' tutted Thelma, who had also arrived. As she waggled a finger, a few pond fronds fell from her fringe. 'How can you innocently serve this poor old lady cups of tea and expect rewards after what you've done?!'

'But I didn't expect a reward. That's what I was saying.'

'How could you even *think* of writing rude words about sweet Nanny Nuckey?' squawked Peggy Pickle.

'I think you must be mistaken, dear,' chuckled Nanny Nuckey. 'I can't imagine someone as kind and thoughtful as Martha writing rude words.'

'Follow me and you'll see just how kind

and thoughtful she *really* is,' said Thelma Tharton. 'After making all that mayhem in our shops, she must have run down here to meddle with yours.'

'I'm sorry you have to see such a thing, but look up there!' said Peggy Pickle, with a dramatic gesture of her arms and considerable satisfaction in her voice.

'I see,' said Nanny Nuckey, gazing up at the rude words

Nanny Nuckey wears knitted knickers

that were still on FULL SHOW right across Raspberry Road. She peered at Martha through round wire spectacles, without moving a muscle. Martha felt like she was being inspected by a top investigator, which wasn't that far from the truth — Nanny Nuckey had been a chief detective until her retirement in 2010. She looked from Martha to the sign and then back to Martha. Then she looked from one tree to the other and then back to Martha. After what felt like an eternity, Nanny Nuckey patted Martha's arm.

'This doesn't have anything to do with you, does it, dear? I wasn't a top detective for that many decades without learning a thing or two about such matters. I don't know about your particular cases, Miss Pickle, Mrs Tharton, but I can say for certain that Martha did not erect that rude sign.'

'How can you be certain?' asked Thelma Tharton.

'Because look how high the trees are, dear. How could someone as short as Martha have got up there without the aid of a ladder, of which there is no evidence, or without an extremely tall accomplice?'

'Blimey! That's an interesting advert, Nanny Nuckey!' It was Jack, who'd just left his dad's butchers to begin his journey to school. 'And what's all this about an accomplice?'

'Is that a confession?' asked Thelma Tharton, who was rather enjoying feeling like a top detective herself, what with asking all these probing questions. 'Are you Martha's accomplice?'

'Think it through, Thelma,' said Nanny Nuckey, with a slow shake of her head. 'Does this young man look tall enough? And do you think either of them are likely to be such quick-fingered weavers?'

'Maybe he provided the ladder. Maybe they bought the sign. I don't know.' Peggy Pickle shrugged. 'Anyway, like you said, you can't speak about what happened in our shops, and there's plenty of evidence that Martha *was* responsible for those misdemeanours. May we use your telephone, Nanny?' she asked, before turning to Martha. 'I think it's time you went to school, don't you?'

'Let's go, Jack,' said Martha, feeling like a punctured balloon, and so they left.

'I suppose it's good Nanny Nuckey doesn't think we have anything to do with that sign, but what exactly happened with Peggy and Thelma?' asked Jack.

'Oh, Jack, it's awful! The ghoul has been making all kinds of mischief, and I'm getting blamed for it. Who knows what it might be doing right now? I was too busy rescuing Nanny Nuckey to see where it went. I know I sneezed the ghoul from the gate, but it isn't fair that Peggy Pickle thinks I messed up her parlour and gave her a bushy beard over her whole face. It isn't fair that Thelma Tharton thinks I spelled out rude words with her flowers and deliberately pushed her into the pond, and –'

'Wait a minute!' said Jack. 'Do you think the ghoul would do something like wrap a scarf of sausages around my dad's neck? He said he was half-strangled by a string of them yesterday afternoon. Me and Mum thought he was winding us up, but maybe it really did happen.'

'That sounds *exactly* like something the ghoul would do,' Martha agreed. 'I just hope The Plan works before even **MORE** damage is done.' She gestured up Raspberry Road at the piles of soil and broken pots, the heaps of hair and the giant woolly sign.

'Blimey!' Jack grabbed Martha's arm. 'Did you mention a plan? What did your gramps come up with?'

'Actually, I came up with it myself after

doing some research and seeing Helga-Holga's jewels and Gramps's wheelbarrow and . . .' She paused. 'I'll tell you later. There isn't time now. We should get to school. I don't want to get into trouble with Miss Parpwell as well as everyone else. We'll put everything into action at the Halloween party. Gramps was really helpful though,' Martha added. 'He even made me scrambled eggs to celebrate coming up with the idea.'

'I'll help you too,' Jack promised, linking arms with Martha. 'By the way, I know *you* like your eggs scrambled, but how do *ghouls* like their eggs?' he asked, with a cheeky grin. 'Terri-fried. That's how ghouls like their eggs. Terri-*fried*.'

IS

In which Martha Mayhem is Marched to Trumpton Town

News travels faster than the speed of light in a place like Cherry Hillsbottom (especially when Peggy Pickle has access to a telephone), and by the time Martha Mayhem and Jack Joke reached school, word had already spread of the COMPLETE CHAOS the ghoul had created in the parlour, the florist and the knitting shop that morning. They arrived to find a notice fixed to the front gate.

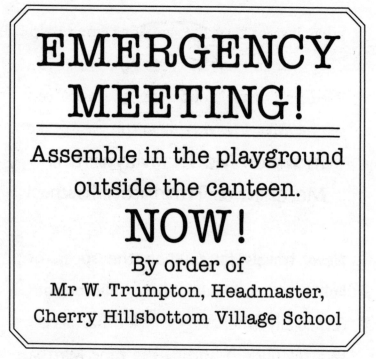

EMERGENCY MEETING!

Assemble in the playground outside the canteen.

NOW!

By order of
Mr W. Trumpton, Headmaster,
Cherry Hillsbottom Village School

'Uh-oh,' said Martha Mayhem. 'They're calling it an emergency, Jack. **An Actual Emergency**. See, I *said* things were serious. What if Miss Pickle called to say I wrote the rude words?'

'Try to stay calm,' Jack comforted. 'I

know it's not easy, but worrying won't help. That's what Professor Gramps would say. Well, he'd probably say, *"Worrying won't help you, my Wonderful Walrus!"* or something like that. Come on, let's see what's going on.'

They rushed round the back of the school to the playground just as Mr Trumpton was about to make an announcement. With a frown on his face, he cleared his throat.

'Due to the unusual winds that are wafting through our village like a whirlwind, school has been suspended.'

'Unusual winds?' scoffed Miss Parpwell. 'I think we all know who's behind this, Willy.' (Willy was Mr Trumpton's first name.) 'I don't know how, but this *must* have something to do with that May girl. It wouldn't surprise me if she and that mad-professor grandfather of hers have made some kind of wind machine that she used to mess up the salon and flower shop.'

'Now, now, Miss Parpwell,' replied Mr Trumpton, his voice lowered so only she could hear. 'We mustn't make willy-nilly accusations.' He cleared his throat and addressed the whole playground. 'I can

assure you that we will get to the bottom of this.'

'Yuck!' Jack nudged Martha. 'I'm not sure I want to get to the *bottom* of anything!'

But Martha was too distracted to laugh. In fact, she'd been distracted by the sight of a great, grey cloud swooping behind the assembled crowd. 'Here we go again. What will it do this time?'

'Pupils, you will spend today tidying up our pleasant village,' continued Mr Trumpton. 'The streets must be cleared of soil and broken flowerpots. The trees must be returned to their wool-less state. You will also ensure that Nanny Nuckey is supplied with a constant stream of tea. The Halloween party will only go ahead if order and neatness are restored to Cherry Hillsbottom before dusk. I repeat: no neatness, no party.'

'Oh no!' breathed Martha, not sure how she could prevent what was on the verge of happening. The mischief-making ghoul had caught sight of Sally Sweetpea's pink hair ribbon and, seizing an ideal opportunity for fun, it was

currently swooping
towards Sally faster
than an Olympic
gold-medal-winning
swooping swallow, if

swallows held Olympic Games.

'Ow!' screamed Sally Sweetpea. 'Who's pulling my ponytail?'

Then, in an unexpected move, the ghoul untied the ribbon, shoved it in Martha's hand and forced her to swish it right in Sally Sweetpea's face.

'Stop it, Martha!' screeched Sally Sweetpea. 'What are you doing? Tell her, Miss Parpwell.'

'I can't stop!' cried Martha. 'I can't control my hand!'

Just then, the ghoul lost interest in Sally Sweetpea's hair ribbon and released Martha's hand. The reason it lost interest in Sally Sweetpea's hair ribbon was because it had found a new interest, in the form of Miss Parpwell's shiny pearl necklace. It whooshed towards the mean-mouthed teacher, dragging Martha with it.

'Yikes!' cried Martha, struggling to stop her arm from grabbing at Miss Parpwell's pearls. 'I can't control it! It's going CRAZY!'

'Mr Trumpton!' shrieked Miss Parpwell. 'Will you take this mayhem-making girl to your office?'

Fortunately, Miss Parpwell's and Sally's shrill shrieking was too much for the ghoul.

It slunk away, leaving Miss Parpwell's shiny pearls intact. Unfortunately, Martha could see Mr Trumpton striding towards her.

'I guess I'm in real trouble now,' sighed Martha. 'See you later, Jack. Let's meet at Tacita's Tearoom.'

After being marched through the corridors by Mr Trumpton, Martha entered his office with a hand over her nose, in case it really did smell of foul fishiness and rotten rats and mouldy mice because he did tons of trumps (she could see his trumpet on the desk, so it was almost certainly true).

'Martha May, isn't it?' asked Mr Trumpton. 'What do you have to say for yourself? What on earth just happened?'

Forced to uncover her nose, Martha sniffed the air cautiously. To her relief, Mr Trumpton's office did NOT stink of foul fishiness and rotten rats and mouldy mice. In fact, it smelled of fresh flowers, and Martha reminded herself not to believe everything she heard before checking all the evidence for herself, as she hoped Mr Trumpton would do.

'Miss Parpwell *thinks* I pulled Sally Sweetpea's ponytail and swished her ribbon, and she *thinks* that I deliberately tried to pull on her pearls.'

'Are you suggesting that you were not responsible for those incidents? Are you implying that Miss Parpwell *mistakenly* thinks they were your fault?'

Martha paused before answering. She didn't want to lie, but she also couldn't tell the whole truth. To tell the whole truth would mean revealing that it was, in some way, her fault because she was responsible for releasing the ghoul from the gate.

'Well?' demanded Mr Trumpton.

'Well, I'm not *exactly* responsible.'

'What's that supposed to mean?'

'I mean, the ponytail and pearl pulling just sort of happened.' Martha shrugged.

'I've never heard of anything happening without a clear cause.' Mr Trumpton frowned. 'And then there's the disturbing matter of the wind behaving in such a peculiar fashion. I've never heard of that either.'

'Neither have I,' Martha agreed. 'Until today.'

'Hmm, yes. Until today.' Mr Trumpton stood up and gazed out of the window with a misty look in his eyes. 'The world has gone bonkers. Or at least, Cherry Hillsbottom has.'

'You look like you need to relax, Mr

Trumpton,' Martha observed, seizing the opportunity to change the subject. 'You should do something nice, like eat scrambled eggs or have some chocolate milk. Or . . . or . . . maybe you should go for a walk. My gramps says being outside is good for clearing the mind, and he's right about most things.'

'Do you know something, Martha May?' Mr Trumpton smiled. 'I'm going to take your advice. I am going to do something nice. I'm going for a walk with my trumpet.'

'That's a great idea, Mr Trumpton, but what should I do? Shall I wait . . . ?'

But Mr Trumpton was already on his merry way, tooting on his trumpet, and Martha was faced with an **Enormously Difficult Decision**: should she wait here until Mr Trumpton returned, or should she seize the opportunity to leave now, so she could finish preparing The Plan? After spending AT LEAST seven seconds considering her options, Martha Mayhem decided to leave. It had to be worth the risk.

16

An Explosive Interlude

'Surprise!' yelled Martha, bursting into Tacita's Tearoom.

Jack almost jumped out of his skin. 'Cripes, Martha! I thought you were the ghoul. What are you doing here? Did Trumps let you out early?'

'Not *exactly*. He left me alone in his office. He didn't say I could go, but he didn't *actually* tell me to stay either.'

'Well, I hope you don't get into any more

trouble. The ENTIRE village is blaming you for what happened this morning.'

Martha gulped. 'Then it's just as well I sneaked round the back of Raspberry Road. I didn't want anyone – or any*thing* – to see me. I'll just have to put things right, won't I?'

'Is that you, Miss Martha?' called Tacita Truelace through a swirl of green smoke. 'All this frothing and foaming is making it difficult to see.'

The sisters had run out of space in the basement, so now the entire tearoom had been transformed into a hubbling, bubbling muddle.

There were tangy tonics in the teapots and pongy potions in the pie dishes. There were mad mixtures in the mixing bowls and fizzing fusions in the fireplace.

'I'm sorry to say that *none* of these spells are going to work, Miss Truelace,' said Martha. 'Professor Gramps and I found out LOADS of fascinating facts about ghouls from gates, including the fact that no known spells work on them.'

'Oh,' said Tacita Truelace sadly. She laid her ladle aside and mopped her brow with a flowery napkin. 'That is a disappointment. I suppose we could try to create a spell that's *not* known, but I've been having enough trouble trying to remember the ones I used to know.'

'Don't worry, Miss Truelace,' said Jack. 'Martha has a plan!'

'That's right, Jack. I *DO* have a plan.' Martha beamed. 'Do you remember what Sally *Sour*pea is dressing up as for the party?'

'A princess?' Jack replied, wondering what that silly girl's costume had to do with The Plan, or with anything, for that matter.

'Exactly — a princess, which is perfect for my plan!'

'What ARE you wittering on about, Whirl Girl?' twitched Griselda Gritch from the comfort of her sister's squashiest armchair. 'I've had it with this nonsense. I'm going to get Helga-Holga right away and fly home to my castle.'

'You are NOT!' Martha insisted. She'd had quite enough of Griselda's unhelpfulness. 'Helga-Holga is a HUGELY important part of my plan, and I'm not "wittering on" about *anything*. I'm putting things right. Why don't you STOP being so LAZY and start helping?'

'Lazy? *LAZY?*' exploded the witch. 'How many witches of my advanced age take tours of the world? How many creatures – witch, human or otherwise – take in orphaned hogs? How many creatures help their sister fulfil a lifelong dream of running a tearoom? And how many have devised a magical means of travelling in puffy polka-dot pants?'

Martha wiggled her nose. 'I was just saying . . . I mean, I just thought we should work together. Everyone's blaming me for *everything*, and I'm trying as hard as I can to put things right. I think your flying puffy polka-dot pants are amazing, and they helped us find my gramps, but I did help you out of the ditch. If it weren't for me, you'd probably still be there. And the ghoul would have probably got YOU by now.'

'All right, all right,' twitched Griselda Gritch. 'We'll stay a little longer, and I'll help. But you clearly *are* completely crackers. Although I do rather like crackers,' she added, with the hint of a glint in her eyes.

'Well, if *I'm* completely crackers, *you* are too,' said Martha Mayhem, with the hint of a grin at the corner of her mouth.

Jack Joke and Tacita Truelace exchanged looks of relief.

'Why don't you tell us more about your plan, Martha?' asked Tacita.

'Professor Gramps and I discovered that ghouls like pretty things such as princesses, so I thought if Sourpea were to walk through the gate *dressed up* as a princess, the ghoul would think she was a *real* princess and follow her through, and then we'd just need to puff it back inside.'

'I get it now!' said Jack. 'Very clever, but there's no way Sourpea will agree to being used to trick the ghoul.'

'Don't worry, Jack. I've worked it ALL out,' Martha twinkled. 'Every last detail.'

'Wow!' exclaimed Jack, once Martha had explained every last detail of her plan. 'This is going to be a party to remember! I just hope we can pull it off,' he added nervously.

'I'm sure we can,' said Martha. 'But there's no time to waste. Meet me at Foxglove Field in one hour.'

17

The Ghastly Gathering in Foxglove Field

By the time the sun had set, and Cherry Hillsbottom was back to looking like any other pleasant village (though with extra cherry trees), Martha and Gramps were ready to put The Plan into action. Martha was dressed in her witch's costume and looked almost *exactly* like Griselda Gritch, and Gramps was dressed as a Mad Scientist and looked quite the part in his white coat and big goggles.

Flickering jack-o'-lanterns lit their journey down Lumpy Lane, the frost formed a path of glistening crystals beneath their feet, and the moon was as full and fat as a thick-crust pizza covered in cheese. They stopped at the gate to Foxglove Field.

'I'd better go to the Grisly Games area,' said Professor Gramps, adjusting his goggles.

Tacita and I will keep people busy playing Pin the Eye on the Cyclops and Hide and Shriek. Helga-Holga is in position and in disguise. She wasn't entirely happy when I brought her here this afternoon, but I know she won't let us down. Good luck, Precious Pumpkin. I have every confidence you'll do a sublimely superb job, and I'm here if you need me.'

'Thanks, Gramps.'

Martha took a deep breath as the professor made his way to the Grisly Games area. She could see it was already buzzing with activity. Nathaniel Hackett Crisp Packet had organised a pumpfootkinball match (which was very much like football, only played with a pumpkin instead of a ball), while Sally Sweetpea had started a game of Tell Me How Lovely I Look (which involved Sally Sweetpea forcing the Sweetpea Sisters to tell her how lovely she looked in her sparkly pink dress).

Further down the field in the Foul Food area, Mrs Gribble the school dinner lady was serving Putrid Potatoes with Bloody Baked Beans. She was dressed as Countess Cruel Cook for the evening and, inspired by Martha's mistake in the canteen, she'd fluffed up her hair and tied strands of sparkly purple tinsel to it. The end result was that she looked remarkably like a cruel countess who worked in a canteen and liked wearing glamorous ghoul-shapes on her head.

Just along from Mrs Gribble, Herbert Sherbet was wearing a blood-stained apron as part of his Zombie Butcher costume. He was busy grilling Sinister Sausages on a barbecue, with Jack at his side, nervously waiting for Martha Mayhem to arrive.

'You're quiet, Jack. Not got any jokes for us, lovey?' asked Mrs Gribble.

Mrs Gribble was right. Jack *was* quiet, because he couldn't stop worrying about whether he was brave enough to play his part in The Plan.

'Um . . .' he said, trying to seem normal, which wasn't easy in the circumstances. 'What do you get if you cross Cherry Hillsbottom with loads of baked beans?'

'I don't know, Jack. What *do* you get if you cross Cherry Hillsbottom with loads of baked beans?'

'Very *Windy*bottom, of course!'

'Un-*bean*-lievably funny, Jack!' chuckled Mrs Gribble. 'Do you have any Halloween jokes?'

'Of course,' said Herbert proudly. 'Go on, son!'

Jack thought for a moment. 'Got it! What do witches put on their hair?'

'I don't know, Jack. What *do* witches put on their hair?'

'*Scare* spray! And where do ghosts go shopping for clothes?'

'I don't know that either, lovey.'

'In *boo*-tiques, of course!'

'Well,' grinned Mrs Gribble, 'it looks as if your costume came from the best *boo*-tique in the land.'

'Thanks, Mrs Gribble. I made it myself.'

Jack hadn't been able to decide whether

to dress up as a vampire, a mummy or a werewolf, so he'd come as a 'wolf-mum-pire'. He was wearing fake fangs, to make him look like a vampire. He'd stuck brown wool to his hands and face, to make him look like a werewolf, and he'd wrapped toilet paper around his tummy, to make him look like a mummy.

'Pssst!' came Martha's voice from behind him. 'Are you ready?' she whispered.

Jack jumped. 'Phew! It's you, Martha!' he replied, struggling to speak through his false fangs. They were too big for his mouth and had started to make a weird whistling noise when he spoke. 'So, I just have to wait until Sourpea has led the ghoul to the gate and then I puff it back inside?' he checked, although because of his whistling fangs, it sounded more like 'I wait-eeeee until Sourpea-eeeeee has led the ghoul-eee to the gate and then I puff-eeeee it back inside.'

'That's right,' said Martha Mayhem. 'And I'll shout any further instructions. I'd better get to Paddlepong Pond to get things started.'

'Hang on a minute, Martha,' said Jack. 'You might have another problem.'

'Don't worry if it's the ghoul. I need the ghoul to appear.'

'It's whinier than the ghoul . . .'

'Martha!' came a whiny voice from the other side of the field.

'Come here immediately and explain why you left Mr Trumpton's office without permission!'

'That's all I need,' Martha sighed. 'I can't waste time being told off by Parp Smell.'

Jack thought for a moment. 'Got it! You look *exactly* like the witch from the ditch. Ask her to pretend to be you while you get on with The Plan.'

'You're a genius, Jack. Or should I say *Jack*-ula!'

'You should leave the jokes to me. That's not at all funny,' said Jack, secretly wishing he'd thought of it himself. 'Good luck!'

Martha Mayhem found Griselda Gritch standing on the edge of the pumpfootkinball pitch. From the way she was shouting things like, 'Push forward!' and 'Cover the midfield!' it sounded like she had an excellent understanding of the game.

'I need your help,' said Martha. 'I need you to pretend to be me for a few minutes.'

'Humph,' humphed Griselda Gritch. 'Do I have to? I quite fancy a game of pumpfootkinball.'

'*Please*,' begged Martha. 'You said you'd help. You can play all the pumpfootkinball you like afterwards, I promise. I'll give you a signal when you can go back to the pitch, OK?'

Without waiting for a reply, Martha nudged the witch from the ditch towards Miss Parpwell and scooted off to

Paddlepong Pond to progress The Plan.

'Watch out, you clumsy clown!' yelled Miss Parpwell as Griselda Gritch hurtled towards her. 'Explain yourself. Why did you trick Mr Trumpton into leaving you alone in his office?'

'And why did you torment my darling daughter by pulling her beautiful hair in the playground this morning?' snarled Cynthia Sweetpea.

'Don't be too harsh on her, ladies,' said Mr Trumpton. 'Her advice did me wonders. I feel so much better after my walk.'

'You're too soft for your own good, Willy Trumpton,' tutted Miss Parpwell. 'What do you have to say for yourself, Martha?'

'You're a crotchety thing, aren't you?' snapped Griselda Gritch. 'You look as mean and moody and unpleasant as a stinky old boot that's been left to rot in a stinky old well for at LEAST a thousand years.'

Miss Parpwell's face turned as purple as a plum. 'You do NOT deserve to be at this party. Take off your costume. Every last wart and whisker!' She tweaked the beetle-y bristles on the end of Griselda Gritch's nose.

'Argh-*argh*-ooo-yu-yu-ee**eee!**'

shrieked the witch from the ditch.

'GET YOUR HANDS OFF ME! NONE OF THIS IS **HER** FAULT,

OR MY FAULT. IT'S ALL BECAUSE OF THE **GHOUL**, YOU FOOL!'

Worried about how angry Miss Parpwell looked (not only was her face the colour of a plum, but her whole body was now contorted like a cat that had been sprayed with water), Mrs Gribble gave Griselda Gritch a friendly squeeze.

'Shh now, Martha, lovey,' she cooed. 'Miss Parpwell looks like she's about to explode. Fill your mouth with these before you make things worse for yourself.' She passed the witch from the ditch a plate of Putrid Potatoes brimming with Bloody Baked Beans.

'Eh?' frowned the witch from the ditch.

'Are these juicy red things food?' (This was the first time she'd seen baked beans.)

'You do say some funny things, Martha,' chuckled Mrs Gribble.

While the witch from the ditch was bolting down the Bloody Beans, and while Miss Parpwell's face was beginning to fade back to its usual colour, Martha was making her way down Foxglove Field . . .

She took a deep breath when she reached Paddlepong Pond. The time had come. This was Martha Mayhem's moment to fix things, to put things right. This was Martha Mayhem's moment to get rid of the ghoul for good.

'It's time!' she called.

After a bit of leaf-rustling and twig-crunching and grumbly grunting, something rather magical happened. A silver unicorn emerged from behind a tree, bathed in moonlight and resplendent in a sparkly glow. There was a shiny horn on its head, and a silver carriage at its rear. Well, almost, but not quite . . .

The silver unicorn was actually Helga-Holga, covered in foil and wearing her new, sparkly diamonds. The shiny horn was actually a pair of pointy bellows attached to her head with ribbon, and the silver carriage was actually Professor Gramps's wheelbarrow, also covered in foil. It has to be said that Helga-Holga wasn't entirely happy being dressed up like this. While she was doing her best to maintain an aura of dignity, Martha could tell from the way she'd lowered her head and kept grunting grumpily that Helga-Holga felt somewhat silly.

'Thanks so much for doing this,' said Martha, hoping to make Helga-Holga feel less silly. 'This is one of the most important parts of The Plan. That's why I asked you.' She gave the hog a hug, which made Helga-Holga feel a little less foolish. 'You just need to wait a few more moments before making your grand entrance.'

Helga-Holga raised her head, as if enthused by the prospect of making a grand entrance, while Martha hid behind the tree.

'Sally Sweetpea, Sally Sweetpea!' she called out in her boomiest voice. 'Your wish for a unicorn has been granted by the President of Princess-ania. PRINCESS SWEETPEA, your carriage awaits!'

Then she waited.

18

A Crazy Conclusion
(involving Parpy Pants, Blasting
Bellows, a Trumping Trumpet,
Glamorous Ghoul-hair, Dancing
Dots and Zany Zombies)

While Martha had spent the afternoon
preparing her plan, the ghoul had spent
its afternoon resting. Exhausted by the
mischief it had made for the Whirl Girl
that morning (it had especially enjoyed
pulling Sally Sweetpea's ponytail, although
it had NOT enjoyed being half-deafened
by Miss Parpwell's painful screech), it had

223

found a peaceful tree
in Foxglove Field and
curled up on the highest branch.
This happened to be the very same tree
Martha Mayhem was hiding behind. It was
still resting there when Martha called out
in her boomiest voice:

'Sally Sweetpea, Sally Sweetpea! Your
wish for a unicorn has been granted by
the President of Princess-ania. PRINCESS
SWEETPEA, your carriage awaits!'

'Princess? Must find princess,' said
the ghoul, drifting down from the
tree. 'Where is princess?'

The ghoul wasn't the only one who'd
heard Martha's call. Sally Sweetpea
had too, which was fortunate, because

that's exactly what was supposed to happen.

'Who's there?' asked Sally, looking up. 'How do you know my name? Oh my GOODNESS!' she squealed as her eyes fell upon the silvery vision. Her heart skipped, her stomach flipped, and her head swelled with pride. 'I always knew I was special! I knew I'd get what I wanted!' She raced to the carriage and climbed aboard. 'I shall call you Eunice Unicornia. Parade me around the field **IMMEDIATELY** so everyone can see how special I am!'

Watching from behind the tree, Martha was trying her hardest not to explode with laughter. What a sight they were – Helga-Holga speeding across Foxglove Field, with

Sourpea gripping onto her tiara with one hand and the ribbon reins with the other.

'Get ready, Jack. You know what you have to do. Pull off the unicorn's horn and use it to gust the ghoul into the gate when it passes through!' shouted Martha Mayhem.

'What? I can't hear you.'

'PULL OFF THE HORN AND USE IT TO GUST THE GHOUL INTO THE GATE!'

'Got it, Martha! I'm read-eeee!' Jack whistled. Except he wasn't *entirely* ready. Jack's hands were trembling so much, he was worried they wouldn't be able to pull off the bellows-horn, so he breathed deeply and told himself he was every bit as brave as a buccaneer exploring snake-infested jungles, to try to get rid of his nerves.

But unfortunately, while Jack was trying to make himself brave, Griselda Gritch had mistaken his funny-sounding fang whistles for Martha's sign that she was free to go and play pumpfootkinball. This was unfortunate because, as Griselda ran to the pitch, her sparkly purple shoes caught the ghoul's attention.

'Ditch witch on the pitch,' chanted the ghoul as it flew after her, forgetting all about the princess and the unicorn, both of whom looked less like a princess and a unicorn with every passing second.

During the course of their jumpy journey, Helga-Holga's foil covering had torn and Sally Sweetpea looked more ruffled than a robin in a raging storm.

'Uh-oh,' said Martha, totally terrified that everything was about to go totally wrong.

Martha thought. She thought like she'd never thought before. She thought so hard her head hurt. And then, through her hurting head, Martha realised how she could use the mayhem of this chaotic situation to get The Plan back on track.

'Puff out your pants!' she yelled at the witch from the ditch. 'Fly as fast as you can towards the gate before it's too late!

Get the ghoul to follow you through!'

'All right, all right,' huffed Griselda Gritch. She puffed out her ENORMOUS purple polka-dot pants, rose into the air and sailed towards the gate. As she glided over the Foul Food area, she felt something unusual. It was a puff, but not the kind she was used to. This puff also made a noise that sounded a bit like 'prp-prp', and it smelled.

What is *that smelly noise?* she wondered, unaware that the Bloody Baked Beans she'd gobbled down were a common cause of gassiness.

The gassy puffs gave
her knickers (which now
actually *were* **PARPY PANTS**)
extra power and propelled her even
faster towards the gate, with the ghoul
following close behind.

'That's it! Don't stop!' yelled Martha
Mayhem.

'What?' shouted Griselda Gritch. 'Stop?'
She de-puffed her knickers and, at the
same time, released yet another 'prp-
prp' noise. Unfortunately, the shock of
this unexpected additional 'prp-prp' noise
caused Griselda to lose control of her

knickers. She was thrust back towards the pumpfootkinball pitch and landed on the edge of the penalty box.

'Shoot!' shouted Nathaniel Hackett Crisp Packet.

Griselda leapt to her feet and pelted the pumpkin in the direction of the goal. It soared through the air at an amazing speed and curved into the back of the net.

'You should join the village team, Martha,' shouted Nathaniel Hackett Crisp Packet.

Delighted to be the centre of attention, Griselda Gritch punched the air with her fist. Another series of smelly 'prp-prp-prp' noises erupted from her ENORMOUS puffy purple polka-dot pants as she skidded through the goal to celebrate, with a murky grey mist hovering around her head.

'NO, Griselda!' groaned Martha Mayhem. 'I said DON'T stop. Get the bellows ready, Jack. I'll just have to find *another* way to get the ghoul to go to the gate.'

Jack pulled the bellows from Helga-Holga's head.

'Take your hands off MY Eunice Unicornia!' screeched Sally Sweetpea. 'Wait a minute . . . All her silver has come off. This is foil. This is . . . this is Martha's horrid hairy hog!' Feeling extremely foolish, Sally stamped her feet. 'A princess should **NEVER** be treated like this!'

'Princess?' said the ghoul, remembering

what it had been doing before Griselda Gritch had run onto the pitch. But the princess was nowhere to be seen (Sally Sweetpea now looked more like a scruffy scarecrow than a queen's daughter).

What am I going to do? Martha wondered, looking around Foxglove Field for inspiration. Just at that moment, a beam of moonlight struck the purple tinsel decorating Mrs Gribble's glamorous, ghoul-like hair, which caused an INCREDIBLE IDEA to strike Martha Mayhem's brain.

'Got it!' Martha ran towards the gate and yelled,

'MRS GRIBBLE! PLEASE COULD YOU COME TO THE GATE AS QUICKLY AS YOU CAN?'

At the sound of Martha's yell, Griselda Gritch reinflated her ENORMOUS puffy purple polka-dot pants and soared into the sky to see what the Whirl Girl was wailing about.

'MRS GRIBBLE!'

Martha repeated, yelling even louder this time.

'PLEASE COME TO THE GATE IMMEDIATELY!'

Thankfully, this time Martha's massive yell did what it was supposed to. It attracted the attention of *everyone* in Foxglove Field, including Mrs Gribble (who was already heading towards the gate to see why Martha needed her) and the ghoul (who was already hot on Mrs Gribble's heels).

'Ghoul-friend!' wheezed the ghoul, gazing at Mrs Gribble's moonlit hair, which looked remarkably like a glamorous ghoul.

As Mrs Gribble huffed and puffed closer to the gate, with the ghoul galloping close behind, calling out, 'Ghoul-friend! Ghoul-friend!' into her hair as it went, Martha called out to Jack.

'Start puffing the bellows, Jack! The ghoul is on its way again!'

Jack took a deep breath. This was it. His moment had come. He had to face his fears. The ghoul was gusting towards him at great speed, so it really was now or never. After taking another deep breath and steadying his trembling hands, Jack did as Martha asked and got to work with the bellows, while the villagers of Cherry Hillsbottom looked on in utter shock at the strange sights.

'What on earth is my son doing with those bellows?' asked Sheila Sherbet.

'And what is my darling daughter doing with that disgusting pig?' sobbed Cynthia Sweetpea.

'And why is Mrs Gribble dancing around the gate under that murky mist? She's bringing our school into disrepute,' parped Miss Parpwell.

'And is that your granddaughter *flying*, Professor?' gasped Peggy Pickle, staring open-mouthed at the shocking sight of Griselda Gritch flying towards the gate.

'I knew it!' said Thelma Tharton, with a slap of her thigh. 'That's how she put up the rude sign outside your shop, Nanny Nuckey – she flew to the tops of the trees!'

'Well, one can't deny actual evidence.'
Nanny Nuckey nodded gravely. 'But look!'
she cried at the sight of both Martha and
Griselda at the same time. 'There are two
of them! Does she have a secret twin
sister, Professor?'

'You must be seeing
double, Nanny Nuckey.
Perhaps someone mixed
up your tea with Beastly
Brew,' suggested Professor Gramps.

'Look! *Here's* Martha,' said Tacita Truelace,
with tremendous relief. 'With her feet
firmly on the ground.'

'All right, Gramps?' Martha winked. 'Quite
a party, isn't it? Please may I borrow your
trumpet for a moment, Mr Trumpton?'

Without waiting for a reply, Martha grabbed the instrument and went to the gate. With a tremendous trump of the trumpet from Martha, and a powerful puff of the ENORMOUS parpy purple polka-dot pants from Griselda, and one final burst of the bellows from Jack, the great grey human-shaped mist was gusted back into the gate.

'Ghoul-friend!' it wheezed one last time before vanishing into the wood.

'We've done it! We've actually done it!' yelled Martha. 'You were brilliant with the bellows, Jack. So brave! The ghoul was right by you.'

'Thanks, Martha. It was nothing,' Jack replied proudly. While it hadn't really felt like nothing at the time, Jack felt amazing now he'd actually done it! 'I'm just glad everything's back to normal.'

He glanced towards the Foul Food area, wondering if his dad had any Sinister Sausages left. 'Nooooo!' he moaned. 'I spoke too soon. Look at everyone's faces. I reckon we're in BIG TROUBLE.'

Martha glanced around Foxglove Field. All the villagers looked as if they'd seen a ghost, which was pretty close to the truth. They'd seen a ghoul. An *actual* ghoul (not to mention two Marthas, one of whom had been seen flying over the football pitch). And nobody was looking very happy.

'Uh-oh,' said Martha.

'Well—' Tacita Truelace smiled, 'there is a way we can wipe this evening's events from their minds. If you remember, I remember one spell.'

'I remember,' said Jack. '*I* remember that *you* remember your forgetting spell!'

'Bravo, Jack! I just need to recollect the right words.' She closed her eyes in concentration.

'With a biff, baff, boof on Helga's hoof . . .

No, that's not right . . .

When I tinkle my toes on Grizzie's nose . . . No, that's not right either . . .

Oh dear. I seem to have forgotten my forgetting spell.'

'Step aside, sister. I'll take over from here,' said Griselda Gritch. She clutched her messy-haired head and made an almighty screeching noise that sounded something like this:

'Argh-*argh*-ooo-yu-yu-ee**eee!**'

Now in a suitably sizzly state for spell-making, Griselda Gritch took hold of Martha's shoulders and began to chant.

'As dots dance from this dress,
And stripes stream from these tights,
They'll forget all that's happened
On this Halloween night.
With a ting-a-ling
On this chinny-chin,
They shall forget
Every single thing!'

Griselda tapped on Martha's chin, and to Martha's amazement the dots danced off her dress and swirled around the villagers.

Within moments, their eyes emptied of colour and they began to sway from side to side like human-shaped palm trees in a breeze.

Griselda tapped on Martha's chin a second time, and the stripes streamed off Martha's tights and spiralled around the zombified villagers. As the stripes swirled around them, the villagers returned to their usual selves, except now everybody looked a LOT happier.

'I guess this means it *won't* be a party to remember after all!' joked Jack.

'Yes!' beamed Martha. 'It looks like your spell *has* worked!'

'Of course. What did you think would happen? I wasn't awarded Young Spellmaker of the Year 1926 for nothing,' boasted Griselda Gritch. 'Just took me a bit of time to get back into the swing of things. And now my work here is done, it's time for us to head home.'

'So soon?' Martha felt as flat as a drink that had never been fizzy. 'Can't you stay just a little longer?'

Before Griselda Gritch had a chance to reply, Helga-Holga stuck her snuffly snout in the air and released a series of peculiar pained moans that sounded something like this:

Aaquwwwww— oOooooh— aaahhhooo ww!

It was almost as if she were trying to tell Griselda Gritch that her Lonely-itis would return if she were parted from Martha. Everyone's eyes fell on Griselda Gritch as they waited for her response.

'All right, all right!' she said eventually. 'We'll stay. For a bit.'

'Don't force yourself,' huffed Martha. 'I thought you might like to.'

Just then, another series of peculiar noises erupted from several directions at once – Professor Gramps's hooting, Jack Joke's chortling, Tacita Truelace's tittering and Helga-Holga's honking.

'What's so funny?' asked Martha and Griselda at EXACTLY the same time.

'You two,' chuckled Tacita Truelace and

Professor Gramps (also at exactly the same time).

'You're almost as alike as two peas in a pod,' chuckled Professor Gramps.

'Or a pair of wiggly witch twins,' added Jack.

'She is NOT a witch,' twitched Griselda Gritch. 'And we only look alike because she copied my clothes.'

'I did NOT copy you,' Martha insisted. 'I had this costume before I knew you existed. And I don't even look like you any more. Look! You made my spots and stripes fall off, so you owe me something.' Martha thought for a moment. 'How about you take me for another ride in your ENORMOUS puffy purple polka-dot pants?'

'Come on then,' huffed Griselda Gritch. 'But only for a few minutes.' She led Martha to the far edge of Foxglove Field, away from the villagers.

After a few paces, Griselda felt a tingle in her left nostril. Then her right. She scratched her nose and sneezed an extraordinary sneeze. It was the kind of sneeze that feels like your nose might blast off and end up at the outer edges of the universe.

'Uh-oh,' said Martha. 'You know what happened the last time someone sneezed like that?'

'I do.' Griselda Gritch grinned. 'And just think how bored we'd have been if you hadn't?'

The witch from the ditch billowed out her ENORMOUS puffy purple polka-dot pants to a tremendous size before she and Martha sailed up, up and away towards the fat, creamy moon.

Look out for
more adventures with
Martha Mayhem
coming soon!

Martha Mayhem
Goes Nuts

Martha accidentally drops a nutmeg
into a 'grow and move' potion concocted by
Griselda Gritch ... Mayhem unfolds when a
magical nutmeg lady appears – and she is
even grumpier than Griselda Gritch!